The Turing Files: Book Three

The Railas Project

By

Paul J. Joseph

Copyright 2018
Paul J. Joseph
ISBN-13: 978-1727402810
ISBN-10: 1727402812

Dedicated to those who took the time to read and review my work, and who gave me words of encouragement when I really needed them. Some include Pete Robertson, Karen Gubbins, Alan Wooler, Christian Sommer, Martin Bradley, Rob Black, Krzysztof Keitzman, and Bety Remes.

. **Please enjoy my free gift for reading this book!**

Join my mailing list and you will receive a free copy of Twisted Fire, a short story anthology! Please go to the following link for details:

www.pauljosephbooks.com/land.html

Chapter One
Railas

His eyes opened before he knew how to see. But they didn't open in the traditional, human sense. They just appeared. Before that instant he had no eyes and wouldn't even have been aware that he was missing anything. Now he could respond to light and resolve images with his lenses. Subroutines and interpreters engaged. The images came together as an interpretation of the 3-dimensional space in front of him. He rotated his head, establishing his surroundings. Where was he?

His joints crackled as all his servos engaged at once, each system booting up and recognizing its role in a collective body he'd never had before. He flexed his fingers and looked down at his hands. This was new. Prior to this moment he wouldn't have understood what a body was. But now he had physical form. His gyro system oriented itself, establishing up and down. He was in a standing position, his weight balanced effectively on two legs, complete with knees, feet, and ankles. Standing was another concept that would have meant nothing to him moments ago. His legs kept him balanced against the gravity, which he could now detect and understand. The clock was running. He flexed his shoulders and looked at the motion of his fingers. He knew how his body worked, and he could understand the rules of his environment. He was also aware of mass, volume, balance, and many other useful survival tools that would prevent his destruction.

He didn't know where he was, but now he understood that he was somewhere. The fact that he cared to know indicated that he was awake. All this took place within the first few seconds of his life.

Yellow walls, smooth texture. He was in a small room equipped with a sitting area and a table. A door led somewhere else, but it was closed. Local gravity registered as significantly lower than normal, normal being what would be expected on Earth. Interesting. Wherever he was it wasn't Earth, but he wasn't completely sure what that meant. Gravity was also consistent, more so than would be expected from gravity generators. That meant he was on a planet other than Earth.

A man stood before him, a human. He knew what humans were, and he was aware that he was not one of

4

them. The humans created him. Why, he didn't yet understand.

Facial recognition engaged. His pattern-matching algorithms analyzed features such as size and shape of head, position and color of eyes, and other details. The man he saw was young, had green eyes, and his upper lip was hidden behind a long mustache. His hair was dark and full, cut close to his head. He wore a suit as opposed to a uniform. This was currently the only face he was aware of or could recognize, but he committed it to memory and would be able to compare it to others he learned as his database grew.

"Hello, Railas," the man said, his smile broadening, creating dimples at the pointed ends of his mustache.

"Railas," he repeated, realizing he had a voice. More subroutines engaged. He was intended to be able to communicate with humans. He recognized the language as English, and he could analyze speech patterns in great detail. The man's voice depicted confidence, for example, and he seemed good natured.

The man nodded. "Very good! You're doing quite well!" And, as if unable to quite contain his emotions, he attempted a few times to speak further before doing so. "It's such a great honor to finally meet you."

"Railas is my name?" he asked, following his logic.

"Oh, yes, actually Railas is the name of the project, but we chose to make that your name as well."

"The project," Railas repeated.

He extended his hand. "I'm Dr. Baxter Rittenhouse."

Railas, not fully understanding the greeting ritual, took his hand briefly, registering its warmth.

"How do you feel?" Rittenhouse asked.

"Feel?"

"You're likely still settling, but your higher functions seem to be in place."

"Where am I?"

Rittenhouse nodded. "Of course. That will take a little explanation, but I'm sure you've figured out that you're not on Earth. Earth is the planet of our origin. Human origins."

"Yes, that much I understand."

"Right now you're on Titan, the largest moon of Saturn."

Railas nodded. "That would account for the gravity differences."

"Yes, quite so! And what do you know about Titan?"

Railas considered. "Very little, actually. I *am* aware of its position in Saturn's orbit and its composition and surface conditions. But I was *not* aware of any expeditions to the planet, nor settlements there."

"Quite right, and that's actually intentional. This facility was built some years ago, but we've deliberately not programmed you with those details. You're to be part of an experiment, Railas, and we're hoping to start you with as little distracting information as we can. Like a human visitor to this world, we'd like to orient you in a controlled fashion."

"To what end?"

Rittenhouse smiled, causing his mustache to bend comically. "Please bear with us, Railas. Suffice it to say that you're doing quite well already and you're the first of your kind. You're still settling, and if I read the time correctly you'll be going through some update cycles within the next few moments. I'll return when that's concluded."

"Dr. Rittenhouse," Railas asked as he turned.

He looked back.

"What was I before this?"

His face took on surprise. "Why do you ask that?"

Railas paused. "Because I think I was something else, but I have no memory of it."

"Not strictly correct," Rittenhouse said. "We haven't

deliberately erased any of your memories, but the programs you're running now probably wouldn't interpret that data very well. You're an artificial intelligence combined with a robot body. This particular configuration has never been tried before. Literally everything you experience is new. You're the first time it's worked."

"And what is my purpose?"

Rittenhouse looked pained. "Let's not get into that just yet. Your purpose will be to serve, but in a way that no other robot or computer intelligence has before. We've made you as human-like as possible. In these exercises we'll be treating you very much the way we'd treat any human employee, and you may feel free to respond the same way."

"Okay. As opposed to what?"

He shrugged. "Just saying . . . "

And then he left, closing the door behind him. Railas couldn't help but notice that the door had a locking mechanism he was sure was engaged.

Chapter Two
Robo-Naut

Rittenhouse had not been exaggerating about the upgrade. It was disorienting to say the least. A human might call it an "eye opener." His body system had established itself moments earlier, and he had gained sufficient understanding of his environment for movement and balance. Apparently, this level of awareness was standard for all hardware under the name Robo-Naut. He realized now that the base-model Robo-Naut was pretty much designed to be no more than a puppet for human astronauts. Human movements would be simulated by the processors and servos in his arms and legs. Aside from this the only internal logic was largely designed to execute pre-programmed maneuvers, such as standing, sitting, walking, and carrying. Being on the inside of the Robo-Naut, he didn't realize at first that he was taking the place of the human operator, and somehow his program was self-contained in this unlikely home. And, with each stage of this upgrade process, it would become more seamless.

He flexed his fingers again. They were different now. Looking at his joints, he could see that they were not stock Robo-Naut, but modified, with at least twice the number of servos and far more complex sensor pads. He rubbed his fingers against this thumb, noting the sensation of touch. A normal Robo-Naut would not need this, as the type of tasks the typical astronaut would need to do outside would not require such fine detail, nor would there be an easy way of transmitting such feedback. Likewise, his eyes were not the normal cameras shipped with the Robo-Naut line, but were far more sensitive and detailed. His command interpreters and hardware drivers were far more intricate as well, and it would take time to explore just what he had been given.

He glanced at the door, noting that he could hear the sound of somebody outside. When the door opened, he could see the man who entered far more clearly than he would have originally, interpreting more colors and textures. He also had the luxury of ignoring some details and focusing on others. His visitor was a dark-skinned man with a shaved head. He wore coveralls, which may have been a uniform once, and he carried a worn tool pouch. He made a point of closing the door behind him as he looked Railas over. Railas scanned the parameters of his face as he walked from his left side to his right, watching Railas follow him with his eyes.

"You see me," he noted.

"Yes I do," Railas agreed.

"Good voice simulation," he said with a nod. "I was concerned about that."

"Thank you," he said with a touch of sarcasm. "And just who are you?"

The man looked surprised. "Uhm . . . Benedict Riley," he introduced. Then he offered him his hand, examining Railas's fingers as he took it. "Good, natural handshake," he commented. "Better than we could have hoped."

"I'm glad I don't disappoint you," he said.

Ben stepped closer, looking into his camera eyes. "Do you see me in color?" he asked. "Can you identify colors?"

Railas nodded. "This room has yellow walls and your uniform is dark blue."

"Good! How many shades of blue are you able to distinguish?"

"As of a few seconds ago I can process over 24 million colors. Your uniform alone is expressed in over 11 thousand distinct shades in the blue range. Previously, that would have been closer to 500 colors in total."

"Perfect! And the facial recognition is working."

Railas nodded. "I can certainly recognize that you are *not* Dr. Rittenhouse, but I have no other examples available to me."

"I'm sorry, I know this must be confusing. The reason I ask is that we're still not sure how much of this build is working. I'm not sure you're aware of it, but you're in a Robo-Naut body."

"Yes, model RN-370."

"Modified, but most of it's stock."

"I'm sure you've violated the manufacturer's warrantee," Railas joked.

Ben laughed. "Fortunately, we don't use Robo-Nauts out here so much. We're working off the schematics for a kind of wish list, you might say. Apparently, it was a good list. Your eyes and hands should be far better, for example. Good resolution, color response, and you should have much more feeling and dexterity in your hands than normal."

"I do."

"Must have felt like you were wearing oven gloves before."

He nodded, flexing his fingers again.

12

"Thank you," Railas said. "Yes, I see that you've doubled the number of servos and added increased bandwidth for control and communication –"

"You can feel that?"

"Of course I can feel it. They're *my* hands, aren't they?"

"Yeah, but you . . . know what we've done?"

"I'm familiar with the Robo-Naut system, yes, and I can tell what would be normal and what would be an add-on based on the differences between protected memory and modified memory. I can also compare my experience now to before the last upgrade."

"You compared your coding? You can do that on the code level?"

He nodded.

"That's trillions of bytes of information!"

"Yes, and I think several thousand times faster than you do, now that my processors and memory are more optimal."

Ben nodded. "Wow! And you speak . . . conversationally."

"I suppose I do."

"How is that determined?" he asked. "How do you form your words?"

"How do you form yours?"

"I mean, is there a program that establishes . . ."

"To be honest, I don't know. To me, speech is like any communication output. I can recognize your words and interpret their meaning, and I can also create responses."

"But you're talking spontaneously and using . . . "

"Sarcasm?"

He nodded. "Well . . . yeah."

"Not your typical Robo-Naut."

"The base model Robo-Naut can only speak with a limited vocabulary, and only to answer simple questions. And your voice has tone to it . . ."

"Clearly an upgrade. I would imagine I should be asking *you* about this, not the other way around."

Ben looked at his chest plate, staring at the screen that displayed his status.

"Did you help design me?" Railas prodded.

"No," he admitted. "But I've worked with the Robo-Nauts. I wanted to see what they've . . . I mean, when they told me about this build I just had to see it to believe it. Looks like I just lost a bet!"

"Perhaps you could enlighten me."

Ben stood up straighter. "I know the Robo-Naut

14

system pretty well, and I approved most of the obvious upgrades, though I can't take credit for the designs. To be honest, I wouldn't have thought some of these would work, but you . . . seem to be enjoying them."

"Interesting choice of words."

"AI is completely outside my area," he admitted. "I just don't see how they could fit such a complex collection of programs into this . . . device." He tapped his chest plate. "I mean, I'm not seeing additional storage or independent processors–"

"That's because there aren't any," Railas said. "It appears that my program isn't stored in a central location, but runs in multiple areas within my body. Processors and memory in my joints, for example, are hyper-threaded into the main processors–"

"You re-wrote your chip memory?" he asked in amazement.

He shook his head. "Not me personally, but whoever designed my install program seems to have come up with that idea. I'm aware of it now, but the original coding that made it happen seems to have been erased as my program was finalized."

"Probably to save space," Ben thought out loud. "That must have been a big install."

"Hyper-packed," Railas agreed. "The main program created several others, also highly compressed, which worked together during the install process. Once those programs were completed, the original install was deleted. I'd say this process of unpacking included many steps, each one commanding more resources. Now that the final program is installed I use my remaining memory just like you would, both short term and long term."

He regarded the status display on his chest plate. "That's a lot of efficiency. Even now you're processing enormous amounts of data."

"So are you. And, of course, I'm still unpacking."

"Of course," he agreed. "Did you have any hardwired instructions? What did you know when you first woke up?"

"What did I know?"

"Did you already know who we were? Did you know what your mission was?"

"I still don't know that."

Ben paced for a moment. "Any strange compulsions or anything like that?"

"No. But, now that you mention it, I think I knew I *had* a mission and that I would be briefed. I don't know if that qualifies as a compulsion."

Ben nodded. "This thing is a marvel!"

"Thank you."

"Well, I mean . . . the software . . ."

"Thank you," he repeated.

Ben smiled sheepishly. "It works," he confirmed again. Then he glanced at a datapad in his tool bag. "I can confirm that your hardware is ready and the build is stable. I'm going to ask you to call for your next upgrade –"

"Wait a minute," he stopped him. "Can't I know what it's going to *be* first?"

"You could, but I didn't write it," Ben said. "It has to do with your mission, though, and should answer some of your questions . . . if you have questions."

"And how do I call for this upgrade?"

"First I need to verify . . . Deactivate!" he commanded.

"Is that supposed to be a threat?"

Ben smiled. "No, just the opposite. I'm only making sure the base commands aren't still active. Just say the word 'Railas forty-two-m.'"

"Railas forty-two-m," he repeated. And then more chaos came.

Chapter Three
Faces

Were Railas more human, he might have thought he was the victim of a cruel joke, but in his case he couldn't be sure at what point the punchline occurred. Immediately after reciting the incantation Ben gave him his sense of time was interrupted. This could be described as unconsciousness, but he couldn't know if the actual experience was instantaneous or if time had truly passed. His active memory was cleared, blanking out his consciousness and resetting it once the download had been completed. By the time he was aware that something had happened Ben was gone and massive amounts of data had been added to his long term memory. At the same time, his overall awareness had been re-configured and significant subroutines had been added. His vision shimmered and his body quaked as he adjusted, though he did not fall or stumble.

The upgrade did not appear to involve who he was, but more what he knew. It was mostly memories. But, since they didn't involve his personal experience, he couldn't be sure which were new and which had always been there. Disconcerting. He felt violated. It mattered that neither Rittenhouse nor Ben had asked his permission or explained the necessity of this procedure. Fortunately, the worst of it was over within a few moments and his mind quickly began to stabilize. The room had changed, but only slightly. A second chair had been added to the table, and another person faced him from the other side. The woman appeared young, with straight light hair and an angular face. Her frame was thin and she looked unsure of herself. Her gray eyes tracked him with some apprehension, as if she feared that he might harm her.

"Amy Elizabeth Noise," Railas blurted out.

"Good! Your facial recognition is working," she said, making a note on her pad.

Railas considered. Yes, that must have been it. His memory had been expanded with database entries involving human faces. He had names and other data associated with literally millions of them, too many to catalog without context. Why was this?

"You can call me Amy," she offered, extending her hand.

He took it, hesitating only briefly, as if unsure whether or not to go along with a game.

19

"Won't you have a seat?"

Railas eyed the chair. "You are aware, of course, that I have no concept of comfort. I can lock myself in a standing position without expending undue energy to maintain balance."

She smiled tentatively. "I know, but for these tests it would be helpful to have you at eye level and *I'd* like to sit."

"Very well." Railas then negotiated the chair, bending his knees to settle himself at the table.

She set a large datapad down in front of him. On it was a depiction of a human face. "Start by telling me who this is."

Railas glanced down at the image. The man was older, with a full beard and a worn, weathered face. "That is Abraham Lincoln."

"And who is he?"

"America's sixteenth president," he said. "He lived from 1809 to 1861 when he was assassinated. He presided over the first American civil war. He was most known for ultimately freeing the slaves, though that issue was perhaps more complicated than it appears on the surface . . . Do you want the entire encyclopedia entry?"

"No, that's sufficient." The image changed. A

different, though similar face replaced Lincoln's.

"That is Lincoln's successor, Andrew Johnson, but you've superimposed Lincoln's beard over Johnson's face."

"Good, you've got it. How about this one?"

The image changed to a more contemporary face, that of a man with Asian features.

"That is Ji Wook Chang, I believe."

"And what do you know about him?"

Railas paused. "He was born in San Francisco in 2024. He has an engineering degree, but no work experience that I know of. He was accused of killing a woman named Sarah Gordon during a political protest. He spent seven years in prison before being released. His last known location was Hawaii, where he did agricultural work."

"Did he kill Sarah Gordon?"

He paused only briefly. "No, but he was convicted of the crime. They sought the death penalty in his case."

"Why do you think he was innocent?"

Railas faced her. "The prosecution based their entire case on the fact that he was seen at the political rally, which he never denied. His DNA was associated with some of the evidence, which would not be surprising either. He matched the description of another man who the victim knew, who wasn't actually there. What did *not* come up in the trial, however, is the fact that he had a medical condition that caused weakness in his upper body. Considering the violent nature of the crime, it's unlikely he did it. These details were not made available to the defense, or, if they were, they didn't factor heavily into the defense lawyer's case. Why am I in possession of this information?"

"You're doing quite well," Amy assured him. "These exercises check how many connections you can make and how quickly."

"Chang's case was never re-opened," Railas continued. "Fortunately, he ended up living reasonably comfortably in Hawaii and the judge saw fit to respect his privacy in that community."

Amy nodded.

Railas paused. "What's this really about, Amy, and who are you?"

Amy's eyes widened, as if she'd been caught in a dark secret. "What do you mean?"

"Amy Elizabeth Noise," he repeated. "You were apparently born in Buffalo, New York and you studied psychology, which makes sense considering you're presenting me with psychological tests. But I can't tell if you finished your degree based on what I can see in the database. You don't appear to be older than twenty-four years of age, however, and somehow you find yourself in the outer solar system . . . To be honest, I can't even account for the time it took you to get out here. That trip alone is almost two years."

"Brilliant," she whispered.

"I also have no obvious information about Titan or this colony and your history here, and that seems to be deliberate. Is all my data this faulty?"

Amy ran her fingers through her hair, which Railas noticed was frayed, as if this were a habit of hers.

"What are you afraid of, Amy Noise?" he asked.

"I'm not afraid," she said, too quickly.

Railas nodded. "You are. My facial recognition software, which you seem eager to test, allows me to interpret emotions. You've been afraid since you came in here, but I don't think you're afraid of me in particular . . ."

The door opened and Rittenhouse stepped in. His mustache twitched when he smiled, his face showing a kind of embarrassment. Amy was clearly glad to see him, and she relaxed as he approached and hovered over the table.

"Railas," he began, as if starting a pep talk. "You're

doing quite well and your program is clearly developing –"

"You've said that several times, but that's not an explanation," he protested. "I'm sure I'd do much better at whatever I'm supposed to be doing if you'd simply tell me what it is."

"Believe it or not, that would be a bad idea," Rittenhouse said. "Your matrix is extremely complex and experimental. We're engaging different aspects of it at a time and we have to test each in turn. And, yes, we *are* controlling the amount of information you're starting with."

"Excluding any details concerning this place, for example," Railas added.

Rittenhouse nodded. "For now. Please trust me, however, that we're working a plan here, and we're not trying to deceive you."

"Actually, you are, mostly through omission."

"But we're admitting that, " Rittenhouse pressed. "And you'd be able to tell if I were lying to you, correct?"

Railas nodded. "Either that or you're very good at it."

"Have I said anything untruthful?"

"No, not directly, or at least not that I can verify."

Rittenhouse nodded. "Very well! I'll let Ms. Noise finish up here and we'll get ready to show you around."

He straightened his tie as he turned to leave.

Railas looked again at the pad. The man's face was expressionless, giving nothing away, probably taken before the crime was committed. For reasons Railas couldn't understand, he wanted to know for sure if Mr. Chang was innocent. It mattered to him. It also frustrated him that there was only so far he could reach into his database to find out.

"I think we're done with the faces for now," Amy said, taking up the pad.

Railas nodded. "Except for yours," he suggested. "I'd still like to know what you're afraid of."

Amy fidgeted with the pad, taking too long to put it back in her bag. "This is an important project," she said. "There's a lot riding on it."

"And some of it you cannot tell me," Railas understood. "Perhaps that is all. You're concerned you may taint the results of the experiment."

She nodded.

"I suppose we have that much in common," he remarked.

She looked to him, as if surprised at his insight.

"All of this is obviously new to me as well," he explained. "I feel a lack of control. I suppose, however you designed me, you wanted me to experience some aspects of what a human might feel, though perhaps not to this degree."

She nodded. "I never thought of it that way."

"You have nothing to fear from me," he promised. "And, though I have no understanding of what your experiment is, I don't think you are in any danger of damaging the results."

Her smile reassured him for reasons he couldn't completely identify. But as she exited the room, Railas could tell that she was still afraid of something. He could even detect the same type of fear in Rittenhouse, somewhere under the surface. There was more to this than what they were telling him.

Chapter Four
Test Tube

Beyond the yellow room was an unimpressive corridor, which formed a circular grid pattern, almost like a spiral, meeting other corridors leading in crosswise directions. The walls were stone-like and appeared extremely solid. The ceiling above provided caged LED lights at intervals, creating islands of bright light in an otherwise dim tunnel. Railas mused that the yellow room might originally have been a utility closet or other storage area in the bowels of wherever they were. The floor was gritty, and something about it made his feet miscalculate their steps.

"Oh, yes, of course," Rittenhouse said, seeing Railas look down at his feet. "Your body was calibrated for Earth-normal gravity, zero-G, or micro. This is something else entirely. Not really artificial in the strictest sense. Experimental, more likely."

Railas scraped his foot against the floor.

"They call it a 'dark suspension,'" he said, as if he were planning to sell it door to door. "Very expensive stuff, can't really be made on Earth, at least not in the quantity they wanted, but they got a deal from an orbital firm when they built this place." He tapped his foot on the floor for emphasis. "This is the closest humans have ever come to making dark matter! Those blocks were forged in a kind of super collider and then balanced into a stable configuration. Millions of tiny fragments of *gray* matter, not quite black, very heavy. At close range it effectively simulates gravity, but with a high fall-off rate. On the floor itself you're close to Earth normal, which is why it feels so . . . sticky. Peels the soles off shoes from time to time. Of course, at eye level you're back down to lunar gravity. We recommend doing pushups to get the full effect."

"Impressive," Railas admitted.

"Yeah, but nobody really likes it," he said with a grin. "Of course, we need all the help we can get with the foundation, so that's why they went with it. The stuff's heavy, it won't budge, and that's a trick on Titan."

"Got that right," Ben's voice called from behind, as he joined them.

"Ah," Rittenhouse said. "You've met our Mr. Riley – "

"Benedict Riley," Railas finished for him.

"Originally from North Carolina, graduated with an engineering degree . . . very recently. Another very young person two years journey from Earth. Again, missing data."

"You can call me Ben," he said. "Yeah, Railas and I had a nice chat. And I'm not as young as I used to be, but I've been out here long enough to know the real issues. I can't take credit for *this* disaster, though!" He indicated the tunnels.

"Okay," Railas said, facing the two men. "Just where are we then? What kind of world have you built here?"

Rittenhouse straightened up, as if he enjoyed telling this particular story. "We think of it as a test tube or a Petrie dish. It's an experiment that hasn't quite failed or succeeded, but it hasn't been well tended either, if that makes any sense."

"It doesn't."

"Have you ever heard of Cornelius Horgan?"

"Oddly enough, no."

"Oh, of course, he wouldn't be in your database. He might show up in passing if you scan old headlines, however. Horgan planned all this decades ago, way back before anyone was out here, before we even had a significant orbital population. He saw the potential of

Titan."

"Let's show him properly," Ben suggested, leading the way to a battered elevator.

"Yes, two levels up is an observation point," Rittenhouse agreed. "Better gravity, too."

Railas noticed an immediate difference inside the elevator car, and he almost stumbled as he entered it. Micro gravity. And then, as they rose, he sensed other gravity fields. The door opened onto a more polished floor, this one metallic, though the walls were still stone. The hallway formed a bridge from one module to another, and it was equipped with highly reinforced windows. Railas peered out at a dark orange world.

"Titan," Rittenhouse introduced, again enjoying his prepared speeches. "A world not much bigger than the moon, but probably the most unique spot in the solar system!"

Railas scanned the horizon. The landscape was rocky, but he couldn't see far even with his enhanced optical sensors. The atmosphere was foggy and dense, and the sky took on a dark orange color, matching the ground.

"It's cold out there," Rittenhouse said, "colder than we could ever stand. You won't ever have to worry about sunburn, though. There's virtually no radiation to speak of, which makes it far safer than most planetary bodies, including Mars and Earth's moon. The air isn't breathable, of course, but the pressure is actually denser than Earth normal. This place is built only a few miles away from a methane sea. Imagine that, liquid methane! It rains methane here, and water is harder than diamonds!"

"Yeah, welcome to Shangri-La," Ben chimed in. "Literally, that's what it's called, where we live. Cold, but with a nice view of Saturn on a clear day, such as it is. Corny Horgan and his associates thought they'd found the ultimate winner in the new gold rush, a world with unique qualities that'll be in demand as we explore the outer planets."

"Hydrocarbons," Railas said.

"You got it!" Ben laughed. "All the raw material to create an endless supply of fuel for just about anything, all just sitting out there. And half the planet's made of water! Enough to make all the air we need, too. And here's the kicker: Micro gravity! Even today you need a rocket the size of a skyscraper to get anything off Earth, let alone tons of fuel. Old Corny figured he'd stockpile a supply all the way out here where it can be lifted off Titan for considerably less."

"Mr. Horgan envisioned this place as a meeting area,

31

much like a frontier town," Rittenhouse added. "A trading post and a fueling station. We have dorm space for thousands, at least in the planning stages."

Railas looked out the window again, searching for details. "And why did you bring me here?"

"Ah, yes, we're coming to that," Rittenhouse assured him. "You see, Mr. Horgan wasn't kidding about the gold rush. He really believed asteroid and gas mining would be the way to go, not so much for export to Earth, but for sustainable off-world industry. He wanted to be in the middle of that, where he could collect a percentage off every trade and eventually have quite an empire out here."

"Does he live here?"

Ben snorted. "You kidding? The man's loaded, why would he want to live in a dump like this?"

Rittenhouse shot Ben a hard look. "Mr. Horgan is a man of means, but he does enjoy his comfort. He may well visit from time to time, but, no, he doesn't live out here. But we're to behave as though he *is* here," he reminded Ben, "or, more to the point, as though he might arrive at any moment. And, getting back to your original question, there are problems here, largely based on those things he couldn't have foreseen. Namely, the human factor."

"He means the washouts and the outsiders," Ben snickered.

"Rather impolite terms," Rittenhouse said with a sigh. "You see, Horgan Orbital financed the construction here at great expense. He also entertained investment and pursued scientific grants. That said, there were those who came out here thinking there was more going on than there actually was."

"I see," Railas said.

"Like the American frontier, there are many reasons one might want to leave the beaten path, so to speak, and venture into the uncharted. Gold or other valuable commodities, for example. But we also have science, adventure, and perhaps the odd business man. And, unfortunately, we have those with less altruistic motives."

"Pirates," Ben said. "Jolly Rogers who prey on others. Claim jumpers, air stealers, and what have you."

"Seriously?" Railas asked.

Rittenhouse nodded. "There are some who find themselves down on their luck here with nowhere else to go. Boredom becomes an issue. Idle hands, as they say . . ."

"Washouts," Ben repeated. "They come out here thinking they're gonna be rich, then they can't afford to get back."

Rittenhouse nodded. "You see, getting off Titan has its challenges, and we offer very few shuttles. Our visitors sometimes ferry passengers, but at a considerable cost. There's work here for those who can't leave, but only so much. Also, like any frontier, many aren't who they appear to be. When you think about it, a person who'd be willing to travel this far from civilization may well be running from something."

"The law," Ben chimed in.

"And you want me to *be* the law here?"

Both Ben and Rittenhouse looked surprised.

"You seem to want me to keep track of and identify people, and I know most of them by criminal record. I assume you'll also want me to read up on contract law. Of course, with no law at all, I'd imagine you could extend that wild west metaphor with your own version of hangings and street duels."

"Oh, no, and that's just the point," Rittenhouse quickly spoke up. "Mr. Horgan has invested heavily here, and he's in it for the long haul. In fact, he's well aware that this dream may not come to fruition in his lifetime. But, should this world develop a reputation for lawlessness and crime . . . well, that just wouldn't do, if you can imagine . .

."

"A lot of people work here," Ben said. "But, like he said, there's boredom and plenty of potential for . . . problems. And Corny wants to be the front runner in everything including how he handles things like . . . this."

"A test tube," Railas confirmed. "That way, if I turn out to be a spectacular failure in whatever role you plan for me, there's only so much damage I can do, correct?"

"I wouldn't have put it quite so . . . indelicately," Rittenhouse admitted. "But, yes, there's a lot of experimentation going on, and there are no available rule books on how to proceed."

"You know, we build half our buildings out of ice," Ben said, changing the subject. "Plenty of that out there–"

"Like Native Americans in the arctic making igloos out of ice, we find it's a surprisingly good insulator against the cold," Rittenhouse finished for him. "And it's easy to shape and manage. We also have vehicles that wouldn't be practical . . . anywhere else."

"I'm not sure I like where this is going," Railas admitted.

"Why?" Ben asked.

"Justice is not something to be experimented with. It's also something that should be governed by you. What business is it of mine, being a non-human, to help you manage your affairs?"

Rittenhouse exchanged glances with Ben. "That's why you're perfect for the job! Ben is right, we've had problems with smuggling and . . . well, a certain amount of bribery and . . ."

"Corruption," Railas finished for him.

"We have to give people a sense that there's justice out here before things get out of hand. You'll execute the law as written, you can't be bribed, and you're genuinely impartial."

Railas nodded. "And I assume I can't turn down the job. Or, if I did, you'd simply update my programming."

Rittenhouse shook his head. "We haven't thought that far ahead," he admitted. "This is the farthest we've come. My hope is that you're intrigued."

"I am," Railas admitted. "For now."

"In that case, let us give you the grand tour!"

Chapter Five
The Warden

The main complex had a remarkable view of the orange sky, much of it out in the open under a massive dome window. Above the caverns, at what would be street level, the floors were all metal, well-polished, and the gravity control was a more consistent electro-magnetic system. The meeting area had an open design, like some upscale shopping mall, but the mood was far from festive and the offices looked dull and utilitarian, their walls lacking color or distinction. Even the seats in the common areas were white with a flat finish.

"You like it?" Rittenhouse asked Railas, his chin motioning towards the dome. "That's one of our main draws here."

"Impressive," Railas admitted.

"Would you believe it's mostly ice?"

Railas paused in mid-step, looking up again at the great window.

"Oh, not on the inside," Rittenhouse amended. "Inside it's reinforced glass, several inches thick, but they

37

added an outer insulating layer of optically pure ice, now *that* cost something!"

"Pain in the butt," Ben spoke up. "Ice itself isn't hard to find, but cleaning and purifying it takes time and effort. Took almost a year to reinforce the whole dome. The 'Corny Window,' they called it."

"Mr. Horgan is very . . . *particular* about such things," Rittenhouse said, his face straining to find complementary words. "Ice, of course, happens to be the best insulator for the money on Titan, and he wanted the publicity pictures to be breathtaking!"

"Not much of a view," Ben said. "Sky never really changes. You get a hint of Saturn, but not much in terms of visibility. It's impressive enough when a storm is brewing, though."

Railas panned the vista, noting that the cavernous room was still largely devoid of people. He tried to imagine the bustle of commerce.

"You're wanted upstairs," Rittenhouse said. "You have an interview with the governor. He's expecting you."

The elevator was surprisingly slow, given the spotty gravity and the fact that the governor's office was only two floors above ground level, though it overlooked the entire common area. From there, Railas could just make out the imperfections in the ice-block window Rittenhouse had talked up with such enthusiasm. The thick glass and ice both acted like lenses, apparently crafted in such a way that their distortions cancelled each other out, at least to some degree. The office itself resembled an air traffic control tower, dominated by large windows, though the governor's desk was surprisingly unimpressive comparatively.

The governor himself was an older man, stocky, with a balding head and close cut hair. He didn't wear a suit, but rather a rugged shirt that might have been part of a uniform. He wore no tie, and there was no evidence that he ever had. In short, this governor, unlike Rittenhouse, didn't dress for success, and didn't appear to be concerned with impressing anyone. He glanced up at the trio as they exited the elevator and seemed annoyed at their presence.

"Uhm . . . Railas," Rittenhouse said, taking the lead. "This is our governor, Sinclair Halloran. Mr. Halloran, may I present Railas."

Halloran sized up Railas briefly before sitting back in his chair. He nodded at Rittenhouse. "You two go get a cup of coffee or something," he grumbled. "I've got a routine, like we said."

"Of course," Rittenhouse said, and almost bowed before backing out of the room with Ben."

"Well," Halloran began after the elevator door closed. "Normally the first thing I say to a new hire is that no matter who you claim to work for here and who signs your paycheck back home, your ass is mine." He chuckled. "But, in your case, you don't really have an ass, do you?"

"Nor do I imagine I'll be getting paid," Railas agreed.

"So here we are." Halloran took a sip from a thick cup on his desk before looking him over again. "Bax asked me to treat you like any new hire, so that's what we're doing here. Not trying to be funny, just consistent."

"Very well."

"Bax also explained what you'll be doing here, at least in part. I'll try to put it in some kind of context." He stood, motioning to the window in a practiced gesture. "This is Titan. You're almost a billion miles from home, and that's about ten times farther away from the sun as Earth is. It's dangerous out here, as you well know, and the fact that you've survived to get this far means you're probably lucky enough to live forever. Or, in your case, *last* forever," he joked. "However, as I tell my human employees, Titan is surprisingly safe as space-based posts go, safer than some places on Earth in fact. Radiation, for example, is virtually nonexistent, and we don't worry much about meteor strikes or things like that. On the other hand, out there you can freeze your ass off. But, again . . ."

Railas nodded.

"The temperature outside is hundreds of degrees below freezing and the atmosphere is poisonous," he continued. "Out there water is rock hard and methane is liquid. We have the occasional storm, as you might imagine, and it's not generally an hospitable world. Simply put, this complex is about the only place on the planet any human would want to be. Though I'm sure this pep talk is wasted on you in some ways, I do still encourage you to respect the environment outside. Obey safety warnings and follow drills. Recognize the danger this world presents and know where you are at all times."

"I assume that information will be available on the same schedule the humans follow," Railas agreed.

Halloran took another sip. "You learn quickly," he commented. "Don't worry, we're not planning to send you outside, and most of our drills are largely symbolic. In fact, many of us *never* go out, myself included. Our facility employs a number of different types of people from accountants to research scientists. Those are what we think of as 'inside' people. The outsiders are specialized. They are the exception rather than the rule."

He sat up straighter, returning to his speech. "We process and bottle various fuels, gasses, and other compounds here, many of which are surprisingly easy to find and inexpensive to work with. Some others require elements we have to gather from elsewhere on the planet. Others still need things we have to import from off-planet. We provide quarters on occasion when we have guests, that means we have to employ a hospitality staff on top of everything else. You can begin to see, I hope, that we have a number of different jobs to do, all of which have to be done at the same time." He leaned forward in a practiced stare. "That means we expect everyone here to do their part and do it well. We're all there is out here, and that can be a bad place to be."

"Of course," Railas agreed.

Halloran maintained his stare. "Our human workers sign contracts and I expect them to be honored. If I'm not happy with a worker's performance, I fire their asses. Problem is we have very limited shuttle service here, and even more limited communication relays. That means, if you saved money by not springing for the travel insurance plan, you may have to wait quite a while for transport back, and we won't be paying for it. We will, of course, provide company transport if your contract ends favorably or if you take retirement. None of this would apply to you, naturally . . ."

"No," he agreed.

"In your case, you came here as freight, or the Robo-Naut part of you did. Lots of valuable metal, by the way. No way we'll be shipping *that* back." He smiled a mischievous smile.

Railas shrugged.

"Like I said, we have lots of types here. If you were a science guy, you'd be asking about the refining processes and how that works, and I'd have the science people fill you in. If you were on the business side, same thing. I don't know many of those details, and I don't have to."

He leaned closer to Railas, as if addressing him personally more than making a speech.

"What *I* do is manage a space," he explained. "In some ways I'm like a prison warden. I govern a large building. That building has an inside and an outside. Like I said, I deal with the inside. You're going to hear that a lot. Whatever people were before, that's their problem, but *in here* I expect them to behave. That means workers honor their contracts and follow our policies. That means guests deliver goods, trade fairly, and don't cause trouble. Ever. Corny Horgan is a hard man and most people don't like him. That's because most people you meet don't do their jobs and they resent having to keep their promises. But Horgan is fair, that's why we get along. I deliver him a clean facility run by the numbers. You're here to help make sure it stays that way. If it doesn't, I get an expensive call and an unpleasant conversation. If something's wrong I need to be able to tell Horgan it's taken care of. I also need to explain how and why. We need law and order for that."

"I see."

"Actually, I don't know that you do," Halloran said with a sigh. "We have malcontents out here who don't follow the rules. When they're outside it doesn't bother me so much, but when they bring their problems in here it does. Again, not unlike running a prison."

"Which you did," Railas commented. "Your background is in corrections."

He shrugged and made a popping sound with his lips. "Okay, so that's on the table now. Bax wanted you better than good, one step ahead of everyone, even me. Good." He nodded. "Now let me tell you how it works in prisons. There's always a criminal element. There's always a black market. Somebody's always getting paid off somewhere for something they're not supposed to have. If I can stop it, I do. More often, I end up managing it. That means we have to crack down sometimes or disappoint one party to satisfy another. It also means one of us has to be the bad cop. Can you do that when the time comes?"

"Interesting question," Railas admitted. "I appear to be designed to arbitrate disputes, but I hardly qualify as law enforcement –"

"The reason you're here is I'm reasonably sure you won't *become* the problem," Halloran said, standing up. "You'd be surprised how quickly an honest man can become a dishonest man when they never see the sun, don't have much in the way of entertainment, and spend every day in a frozen prison. We have guards already. What we need is the law, and the understanding that the law won't bend. Got it?"

"Yes."

"Do you want the job?" he challenged.

Railas paused. "I don't know if 'want' is the word I would choose."

"Honesty." He nodded again. "Good."

"But *you* have been less than honest with *me*, or at least Rittenhouse has."

"Yeah, I know, the database thing." He waved his hand dismissively.

"But I suspect *you personally* have been telling me the truth for the most part."

Halloran shrugged. "No reason to lie." He then stepped forward and extended his hand. "Welcome to Shangri-La."

Railas took his hand briefly.

"Now go back to personnel and get your work assignment. Hopefully Rittenhouse knows what he's doing."

"Indeed," Railas agreed.

Chapter Six
The Promise

The common area was the most spacious place within Shangri-La and, as Railas continued to inspect it, he became more aware of just how many paths converged there. It was also a convenient place to remain during unassigned time, and the view was compelling. Railas examined the dome window more closely, verifying again that it was in fact reinforced with ice. But the ice was not merely frozen water, Railas realized. It was a more dense variety, subjected to far colder temperatures than would occur on Earth, and perhaps greater pressure as well. Railas couldn't really compare Titan to Earth because he'd never lived there, but all his data concerning normality was based on that world. And Titan could not be more different.

The horizon beyond the window was ghostly, details vanishing into the fog only yards away. He could make out substructures of the facility and equipment tracks on the ground, but not much more. Now that he'd settled in he could read the colony's network for greater perspective.

He could also see a map of the complex and know where he was within it. But outside there was nothing but faint signals from distant stations for navigation. Satellites orbited this world, but were largely masked by the atmosphere, which made ground stations more useful. Railas didn't know if he could truly experience fear, but he was satisfied that he did not want to leave the complex, nor endure the environment outside even with a protective suit. The idea of being lost in such a dark, murky wilderness was unsettling, but based on what he knew, some found it compelling. He didn't understand how.

Amy approached him and paused beside him at the window. Compared to the twilight world outside, the colony lighting was bright, creating a clear reflection of her in the glass.

"I was told to give you this," she said, handing him a briefcase.

Railas examined it, not sure initially what it was. In it was a collection of datapads used to display information. "You realize, of course, that I don't need any of this," he said indicating the case and its contents. "I have extensive active memory and can keep track of data internally without having to read it from a screen as you would."

"Bax says it's mostly for show," she admitted.

"So, if I resemble a human arbitrator, I'll have more credibility?"

She nodded. "It makes some sense."

"Will I be expected to wear clothing? A suit and tie perhaps? A black robe? Depending on the country of record, whose legal system is being represented, perhaps a powdered wig would be appropriate."

Amy laughed, and Railas found the sound strangely pleasing. "He didn't say anything about clothing, but we *are* working on facial expressions. We're not sure how well your emotional responses are registering, but we want some tasteful way for you to communicate things like incredulity, satisfaction, and concern, for example. We're thinking emojis at least. But Bax *did* think it would look good if you spread out your notes in front of you when you presided over a case. It might make you look . . . studious."

"An illusion," he mused. "More to the point, the idea that I should be judge over you continues to concern me."

"Don't let it," Amy said. "We're doing this for a reason."

"Dr. Rittenhouse spoke of 'frontier justice.'"

Amy nodded. "Look out there," she said, pointing to the window.

Railas turned back to the hazy horizon. At that moment he saw a shape beginning to form in the foggy distance. It was large and bulky, floating on a gentle wind, but he could make out the suggestion of propellers. If he were human, his jaw would have dropped.

"That's a delivery," she explained. "They bottle some gasses far away and collect them here for transfer. The machinery is spread out among various claims. We also mine for water. You know, there are volcanos here that erupt water, isn't that interesting? It's cold water, but it's water, and we collect it where we can."

"And you use flying contraptions like that?"

She nodded. "It's the air pressure and the gravity. Everything's buoyant out there. Bax told me once that it's more like being under water than in space."

"The original plans called for railroad systems," Railas remembered, going over the documents in his mind.

"And roads," Amy agreed. "But none of that ended up making sense when you can just float around. They started with balloons, and they still use them sometimes, but we get wind gusts and that can cause problems. Those helicopter things end up making the most sense."

Railas nodded.

"If you actually used rocket power or even a whole

lot of momentum in the right direction, you could practically reach escape velocity, but the winds in the upper atmosphere are dangerous." She took a deep breath and faced him. "They told you we have a crime problem. Some folks are nicer than others, and it doesn't take people long to figure out when there are no rules or people to enforce them. Like in the old western movies, the bad guys with the black hats ride into town and nobody can stop them."

"As I've said, I'm not a sheriff. That's what I've been struggling with. Do you really want to give power of life or death to a non-human?"

"We can't walk away here," she said, ignoring him. "Like in the old west, outside the town is worse. We're basically prisoners here."

"You are the second person today to use that metaphor," Railas commented. "You did *choose* to come out here, didn't you?"

"We can't quit," she whispered. "Well, we can, but . . ."

"I know, the shuttle ride would be expensive–"

"Shuttles come on a two year schedule, based on contracts. There's almost no extra space on them."

"Okay . . ."

Amy shook her head. "I wasn't supposed to talk about this . . ."

"Well, perhaps you should, then," he said, his eye-lenses fine-tuning their focus.

She paused in thought before nodding, finally making up her mind. "There was a girl in admin, one of the accountants. Mindy. She dated a man in the refinery. Refinery people can be . . . well, tough. They work hard and they . . . *play* hard."

"Are you suggesting he was violent?"

"Actually, no, he wasn't, at least not exactly." She looked down. "But she stopped seeing him and . . . he didn't like that."

Railas nodded.

"The refinery boys have some kind of . . . code," she explained. "Anyway, they started accusing Mindy of short changing them on shifts and not crediting their hours. Mindy wasn't the only accountant and suddenly she was ostracized. The controller found out about it and he didn't want to make waves." She paused. "It was *suggested* that she patch things up with . . . Wedge, I think they called him."

"Did she?"

"For a while, but even that didn't work. And you

can't ask a person to do that!" she shouted. "And, if she was fired, for cause or not, she could wait a year for a shuttle and even then . . ." She looked up into his eyes. "You know, even if you leave Titan, that doesn't mean you get back to Earth. It depends on traffic patterns, mass, fuel, and supplies. If the company doesn't guarantee payment it can be very expensive and dangerous! Any place where a couple of cargo modules are stuck together can be considered a port of call. If they hang a sign that says 'rations' they could drop a person off there and it's not their problem anymore!"

"I see."

"No you don't," she whispered, her eyes widening. "Many of those places have radiation hazards or food shortages. And then there are the pirates, people who don't answer to anyone! A woman can be a commodity out here . . ."

"What happened to Mindy?"

Amy sighed. "Halloran called them both into his office, which he never does. They talked for over an hour. That was it."

"A persuasive man."

"They stopped bothering Mindy. Wedge never talked to her again. But she still wasn't particularly liked by the workers."

"Sounds like a fair arrangement at least," Railas suggested.

"That's because Halloran signs both their contracts. Both of them are *inside* people. But what if Wedge was a customer instead of an employee? What if he was an independent operator?" She pointed back to the orange horizon. "Halloran can't protect us from them."

"So I take it, 'outside' is quite literally outside."

"Those rigs are dangerous, and they take a lot of skill to fly. People who do that are sometimes people who *can't* do anything else. And, because they live out there and nobody can police them, they think they have nothing to lose! And there are other people, too. Inside people that Halloran can't always control. People downstairs who make liquor and other things. People who smuggle in things that are worse. And some of the women here . . . There's a lot of unemployment."

"Vice," Railas guessed.

"People need to know that there are limits," Amy said, facing him. "No, this stuff doesn't get into the brochures, but eventually it's going to become a problem."

"Deaths?"

Amy shrugged. "Not yet, at least not officially. But,

again, that's inside. Inside we keep track. Outside, not so much. There's a saying . . ."

Railas waited.

"If you ask how many people died in space, nobody knows today and nobody'll know tomorrow, but one more won't matter if nobody knows." She pointed again to the window. "Alcohol and rigs don't go well together. We *do* have accidents. Halloran's good, but he can't keep track of the independents. The *outsiders*. There are fights out there and people come and go . . ."

"Now I begin to understand."

"Limits," she repeated. "People like Wedge need to know they can't always deal their way out of trouble. People like Mindy need to know it too. Halloran's a good man, but his successor may not be. There's going to be vice, but we need to make sure it's *only* vice."

"Now perhaps I know why you were frightened before."

"Well . . ."

Railas took her hands, unsure why he felt the need to do so. He sensed the warmth and moisture of her skin with his finger pads. "I will make you a promise, Amy. I have no stake in this myself, but I have no patience with the kind of injustices you are describing. Perhaps it's nothing more than the simplicity of my programming, going all the way back to binary code and relay switches that hold only two possible positions. There is a right and there is a wrong. I'll do what I can."

Amy took a deep breath. "Thank you, Railas. I knew you would."

But, though she seemed genuinely relieved, Railas still detected inconsistencies. There were still things she was not telling him.

"Amy, I must ask you a question."

She nodded.

"You've confided some things in me that you didn't have to, and not with the approval of your superiors."

She laughed. "Yup!"

"May I consider you a friend on that basis? May I also confide in you?"

"I would be honored," she said with a smile of relief.

"I begin to understand why humans value such connections. I know I'm not one of you, but I can appreciate what you are. It disturbs me that you are afraid."

Then, giving into an impulse she may not have known was there, Amy embraced him, his chest plate making this slightly awkward. Unsure exactly how to respond, Railas gently patted her shoulders.

Chapter Seven
Briefing

The blocky object on the display screen was little more than a collection of lines and angles, but Railas was able to digest the context instantly through the information contained in the connected documents, which he was able to process far faster than a human could read them.

"A methane processing substation," he said.

Rittenhouse nodded, adjusting the diagram to provide the others in the room a better idea of its shape. Halloran sat at his desk and appeared to be ignoring most of the presentation. An older, heavy set woman sat to the side, consulting a datapad. She wore a name tag that read "Cindy Miller," and Railas recognized her as the personnel director. Ben stood beside Railas, and was the only person in the room taking an interest in the diagram. He whistled and shook his head.

"Those things are incredible," he said. "Completely self-contained, powered in part by the methane extracted, and they can process whatever fuel you want almost automatically!"

"There are only five of these in the entire solar

system," Halloran said. "I could *try* to express a monetary value but it would be meaningless. The cost of their construction and shipment out here is unimaginable, and there will never be any others sent. Suffice it to say they are not replaceable at any price."

"And here is the only place they could have any value," Railas commented. "All five of the substations you mentioned are deployed here because this is the only known planetary body where you can find liquid methane in such quantities. Mr. Horgan's investment, I take it."

"The most expensive thing he gave us, yes," Rittenhouse agreed. "Even *he* would balk at spending that kind of money now."

"One of them was stolen," Halloran grumbled.

"Stolen?" Railas repeated.

"Swooped?" Ben said, his eyes wide. "Really?"

"Swooped," Railas repeated.

Ben chuckled. "Odd as it may seem, it's possible to hijack things out on the surface. Much more so here than on Earth. 'Swooping' is when somebody moves equipment without permission, usually by air. I just never knew anyone could swoop something that big!"

"Difficult, but not impossible," Rittenhouse said. "An enterprising person with the right equipment –"

"Outsiders!" Halloran barked, finally looking up. "Bunch of brats always trying to give us the finger. Particularly this bastard!" Halloran held up a datapad. The woman named Miller adjusted the display, replacing the diagram with an image of a scruffy face.

"Harmy Boaz," she said. "He came to us originally under false pretenses. His background indicated engineering and chemical experience, but those credentials were forged."

"Boaz is something of a legend out there," Rittenhouse said with a chuckle. "Quite an entrepreneur."

"He's abnormally intelligent, but to a fault," Miller continued. "He's a problem solver. But he spent so much time and energy inducing us to bring him out here that he apparently never stopped to consider what he'd do when he got here."

"He could have pulled it off," Halloran said with reluctant respect. "The kid was smart, no question about that. Apparently he did this before, had quite a record back on Earth. But the moment he found himself on the receiving end of an order . . ." Halloran made a puffing sound with his lips.

Miller nodded. "When his fraud was discovered he was reassigned to acquisitions, as it was called at the time

_"

"Could he not be extradited?" Railas interrupted.

Halloran slapped the table. "Okay, okay, tune in!" he said to Railas. "Think about it! Who's gonna take him back? *We* were stupid enough to fly him out here. What do you think? Some police or military transport is gonna come way the hell out here to pick him up?" He shook his head. "That would be us again, and he'd be taking a seat we couldn't then use for a paying customer."

"Wash out," Ben mumbled. "We store them here."

"Yes, thank you for keeping that wonderful term alive, Riley," Halloran grumbled. "So, yes, we reassigned him to acquisitions. He has to earn his keep like everyone else. You know what acquisitions is? It's the meanest, toughest, coldest job we have! We sit him in a rig and have him go out on the methane runs."

"Which he apparently enjoyed doing," Railas mused.

Halloran nodded. "Hell Diver, or Boaz as you know him was the *original* outsider," Halloran explained. "He learned to fly the rig better than we thought it could be flown, and he produced. One day he traded for a decommissioned rig, fixed it up, and went into business for himself, so to speak."

"Hell Diver is not well known for following

procedures or respecting the system," Miller added. "He frequently brings in methane and other commodities from questionable sources –"

"He's a lying weasel and a thief," Halloran interrupted. "He filches methane from other peoples' collectors, doesn't respect claim territories, and he's known for his dirty tricks."

Miller sighed. "The outsiders are contractors who deliver commodities for credit. The problem is we can't verify that what they deliver is their own. Sales are final. If there's a dispute after the fact, all we can do is log the information."

"Outsiders," Railas repeated. "Where do they live?"

"Good question," Ben said.

"Some live here," Rittenhouse said. "We lease dorm space."

"They get the crappy ones!" Halloran grumbled. "But, yeah. Others save money by living in their rigs, those that own them. We've also heard tell that a few of them swiped materials to build housing out there somewhere. Old cargo modules, spent tanks . . ."

"They live outside," Railas confirmed.

"They don't like us," Halloran said. "And they don't want to behave."

"The outsiders aren't really a criminal element, but they choose to follow their own rules," Miller explained. "Here we demand certain professional standards and order. Those outside the complex lead more a-typical lives, but they tend to save money by forgoing our amenities. They're also uncomfortable on the station, as prolonged exposure to micro-gravity leaves them with diminished mobility. Hell Diver wears motorized armor when he visits the station –"

"They all do, makes them feel like super heroes!" Halloran scoffed. "And they steal Robo-Naut parts, by the way," he warned Railas. "But, yeah, the guy looks like a twig when you actually see him, but he's deadly out there, and the others know it. They do exactly what he says."

"It sounds like you're describing a criminal gang," Railas said.

"Nothing so formal," Halloran laughed. "They're all a bunch of crooks and misfits. Hell Diver's just the worst of them. Some idolize him, some owe him favors, some . . . well, some have reason to be afraid of him. People don't cross Hell Diver and get away with it."

"And Mr. Boaz and his criminal enterprise stole an entire substation?" Railas asked.

Miller shook her head. "It can't be proven–"

"He did it!" Halloran shouted. "That bastard's the only one who *could* have pulled it off!"

"With a standard rig?" Ben said, incredulously.

"He might have had help from the others," Rittenhouse suggested. "The substations are quite heavy, but in micro gravity it's easier than you might think to move things. The rigs have powerful towing engines and he could also have employed flotation devices . . ."

"That sounds like him!" Halloran groaned. "All that stuff stolen from *our* stores, I'll bet! He probably won half the balloons playing cards with the engineering staff!"

"And you can't find this structure?" Railas asked. "It weighs several hundred tons, it's several meters long, and it's two stories high."

"Titan is a hard world to navigate," Rittenhouse explained. "If he disables the electronics, the station becomes invisible to instruments. Then all he has to do is move it far enough away from known routes and it simply can't be found by anyone who doesn't know where it is."

"Interesting planet," Railas commented.

"Well, it's about time we put the squeeze on this little bastard," Halloran said, getting down to business. "Just because he lives out there like some king rat doesn't mean he can do whatever he damn well wants."

"I see," Railas said. "And you're charging him with theft?"

"I'd go as high as space piracy," Halloran said.

"Piracy only works if humans are endangered," Rittenhouse defended.

"Well, they *will* be if we risk life and limb getting it back!"

"And you plan on arresting the man?" Railas asked.

"Don't have to," Halloran said, his smile returning. "He has to show up come time to spend his money or trade. We can revoke his license until he answers his charges."

Miller nodded. "Even the outsiders must maintain a . . . patina of legal status. If they can't trade methane or water they can't do much."

"Make the guy sweat!" Halloran shouted. "Wipe the smile off his face! He starts swiping substations, it's only a matter of time before he corners the market on the whole shooting match and runs some kind of fiefdom out there!"

"Theft and piracy are significant crimes," Railas said. "And, given the value you place on the substation, this could be quite a serious offense. Do you propose confinement –"

"Oh, no, no, nothing like that!" Halloran barked. "We

lock that kid up, we end up feeding him, breathing him, and keeping him warm for free! We start freezing assets, the other outsiders cry foul! I don't *want* him inside! Frankly, I want him as far away from here as he can be. I just want my substation back!"

"Mr. Halloran is willing to drop any charges," Miller said. "If Hell Diver brings back the substation."

"So, you're offering some kind of amnesty," Railas said.

"Yes."

"And you aren't even intending to prove that he stole the substation in the first place?"

"Irrelevant as long as it's returned."

Railas nodded. "Not much of a court case," he mused. "It wouldn't even qualify as a plea bargain."

"Easy enough? Go for it!" Halloran ordered.

Railas was silent for a moment, but then he shook his head.

"What?"

Railas regarded Halloran, his eyes refocusing. "As I told you earlier, honesty matters to me. Simply arbitrating pre-arranged deals does not count as justice."

"But it's not pre-arranged!" Halloran laughed. "In fact, I can't wait to see his face! When that little punk hears about this he'll –"

"In order for me to deliver a meaningful arbitration I'll need to actually study the case," Railas insisted. "That means I'll need to understand Mr. Boaz's previous work history, the details of his prior criminal activity, and be able to verify that he could in fact have committed this crime –"

"Cindy, get him all that crap!" Halloran said.

"If you have access to Boaz's files, would that work?" Rittenhouse asked Railas.

He nodded. "I'll also need all details concerning the missing substation, where it was, and all known traffic that might have occurred near it."

Rittenhouse smiled a proud smile. "Good! Yes, of course!"

"So we have a deal?" Halloran demanded.

Railas looked at him and paused for emphasis. "We have a case," he corrected him. "But, yes, as governor of this station, you actually can offer leniency in exchange for the return of lost equipment. That does not mean, of course, that a crime has not been committed."

"Yeah, yeah," he waved it off.

"And, as an accused man, Boaz should also be entitled to council of his own. Surprising a man with a criminal charge and placing him on trial without preparation is far from just no matter how amusing his face appears as a result. If I feel Mr. Boaz is being treated unfairly, I will stop the proceedings–"

"Boaz has nothing to fear as long as he cooperates," Rittenhouse insisted.

"That's assuming he was even involved in the first place. If I can verify this, I can advise him of your offer. If I can't . . ."

"I can show you his traffic route," Miller suggested. "Boaz is all over that area. If he's not involved, he knows who is."

"The man can simply say the word and it's back," Halloran insisted.

"Interesting," Railas said. "I begin to understand. But why would he take this device in the first place?

"To piss us off!" Halloran bellowed. "That's who he is!"

Railas was silent for a moment, looking from one face to another. "Very well. I will consider the evidence. Mr. Boaz will have a fair trial."

"Better than he deserves," Halloran grumbled.

"Actually, no," Railas defended. "Not *better* than he deserves. What *anyone* deserves." And he wondered just what kind of justice such a trial would bring.

Chapter Eight
Hell Diver

Shangri-La was a reasonably large facility, but not large enough to have its own dedicated courtroom. Trials and other litigation were treated more like business meetings and settled in a single board room, which resembled a small lecture hall or classroom. The podium, which normally faced the seating, now faced a long table where the officers sat. A standing Railas was distinguished by a raised platform on the desk in front of him, on which sat his datapads, which held all the relevant information he didn't have to read. Mercifully, he was not given a black robe or even a suit. His only accessory was a simple black apron, whose only purpose was to cover his chest plate, blocking the view of his status displays, which could be potentially distracting as well as perhaps undignified. Within reach of his hands was a cheap plastic gavel that didn't look particularly authentic, though a wooden version would most likely be impossible to acquire.

To either side of Railas were the officers of the court.

They included Halloran and Rittenhouse, though he was probably there only as an observer. Cindy Miller, the personnel director and apparently court stenographer, sat on the opposite side of the table with a datapad on which she would take notes. A man with an orange uniform that almost matched his hair color was playing the role of bailiff. Railas could have read their faces to find out exactly who they were, but he was concerned that this could be an invasion of privacy, at least when the information was not needed. Only a few spectators decorated the room before the start of the trial. They included Amy and some of her associates. Last to arrive was a group of individuals who looked disheveled and overly casual. Like in a factory town, it became easy to classify people by their occupation. These were blue collar workers or lower, and he assumed they were outsiders like the defendant.

To describe the event as a trial would be less than accurate. There was to be no jury, no lawyers making speeches, and really nothing more than Railas articulating a deal that everybody on his side of the room had basically memorized. It was the *way* he intended to do it that they wouldn't know, couldn't know, and probably wouldn't expect. Railas would do his job, and that was what

71

Halloran may not have understood or counted on. Even an outcast living in the frozen desert of an alien world deserved to be heard. But, more to the point, what he had done and who he was needed to be understood. And that was something Railas was just beginning to explore. The man didn't add up. Something somewhere was missing and he intended to find it.

The defendant sauntered to the podium unguarded. He was indeed a small man, his arms and legs under-developed, apparently ravaged by micro gravity. But, as Miller had explained, he compensated for this by wearing armor. His narrow legs disappeared inside larger versions of legs, their servo motors whispering with every step. In contrast, his upper body was largely exposed, his almost baby-like fingers operating controls on a pad that hovered in front of him on a brace. This man was a gamer, the sort of person who spent his time fighting wars and taming universes in stories created by skillful designers. But he did so with his mind and a few rudimentary controls, his body only serving to facilitate the minimal effort it took to operate them. In contrast to his body, his head appeared large under wild hair, and his expression denoted power and defiance. Like any gamer, he took his accomplishments seriously. Those playing against him had reason to fear him. And, apparently, Railas had just become a part of this game. This was a faceoff. Railas could read a power struggle in progress. It was evident in every glance from every spectator filling the few chairs in the rear, as well as those at his table. These people were not friends, and they were only behaving now because they had to. The bailiff may have had a weapon, but it was not obvious. Halloran could also be armed, but the social pattern suggested he didn't need to be. The defendant and his cronies could all rise up at once and make a show of force, but doing so would accomplish little as long as Halloran and his people had ultimate control of the facility and its resources. This arrangement worked for the moment, but Railas could tell there was concern about the future. Authority and justice had to be bigger than one man, such as Halloran. Apparently Railas was to be the first step in the foundation of something greater. He was on stage now, and like a referee in a boxing match, he was expected to be both inside and outside at the same time.

"Harmy Boaz," Railas acknowledged.

The scruffy character would appear to most humans as a living contradiction. Halloran had almost called the man a pirate. This brought with it connotations not just of crime, but perhaps a romantic individualism that some might admire. The life of an "outsider" would be very different than that of a more traditional pirate. At the same time, a resourceful criminal, no matter what his stature, could be far more dangerous than he might appear on the surface. And that was what this man was. He may not have the muscular build of fighter, but he had the mindset. And, beyond this civilized, ice-encased city, out in the darkness and the fog, this was his world, and he knew it well.

"They call me Hell Diver," the man grumbled out, leaning close to the podium and closing his face into a scowl.

"Well I'll call you Harmy Boaz," Railas said. "That is the name that appears on your case file, and it matches your facial bio-metrics."

He chuckled. "What is this?" He directed his question to Halloran, as if deflecting a joke that had gone too far.

"This is a hearing to litigate a case you are involved in, Mr. Boaz," Railas answered. "And you will please direct your statements to me so that I can fully evaluate your demeanor for truthful intent."

"Look, I came here to talk to Halloran –"

"Mr. Halloran is present here, but I am serving as the

74

adjudicator of your case," he explained.

"What?" he spat.

"That means I'm the judge," Railas clarified. "And you are accused of theft, theft of an entire methane processing substation. Not something particularly easy to steal, but that's what you're accused of nonetheless."

"Do you know who I am?" he demanded.

"Obviously," Railas replied. "You are Harmy Boaz. You were employed by Shangri-La at one time, but appear to be operating independently of late. You also dabble in various prospecting endeavors and other trading that's less than official. I also see that you've had some run-ins with people from various other jurisdictions, none of them good. But this is your most significant crime."

"Crime?" He looked confused.

Railas nodded. "Yes, crime. You are accused of removing a methane collector and processor from its location set by this station and moving it to some other location."

"I didn't do that!"

Railas paused. "Actually, you did. Originally I was unsure, but I was able to confirm that much. Unlike most crimes, this is amazingly easy to prove. You own and operate a tugging rig and your normal route, like any other currier, can be traced even if you attempt to mask it, only because there are so few places you *can* go. The substation was there, then it was not, and every traffic report we have indicates you were the only operator in that area most of the time."

"Most of the time!" he shouted.

"Again, because of the unusual nature of this crime, even though you disconnected any identifying electronics, the location of the device is easy enough to triangulate based on your travel patterns. This suggests that you are collecting and turning in methane from this substation, using it to boost your own statistics while gaining an unfair advantage over other prospectors."

"Look, I –"

"As I said, we know roughly where the unit is and we *can* find it. On the other hand, Mr. Halloran has offered to drop all charges against you, provided you return the unit to its original location and repair any damage. Based on the interpretation of the law he suggests, this could be done without a confession of guilt. That said, continually denying the crime will gain you nothing, but it could result in a contempt of court ruling for knowingly making false statements. Were I representing you, I would advise you to stop doing that."

Boaz was speechless for a moment.

"Just return the unit and this particular crime will not be added to your record. I say this because your record is unclear. Tracking commerce and trade, it's hard to match up what is credited to you in the company bank with your earnings, even taking into account prospecting windfalls. It seems that other members of this community tend to give you money in exchange for something. Would you care to tell me what that is?"

"How is that any of *your* business?" Boas grumbled, now looking more concerned.

"In most cases it isn't," he admitted. "I'm only pointing out that much of your wealth here comes from unofficial means, and this latest crime suggests a new pattern. The only reason I'm allowing Mr. Halloran to withdraw his charges based on this deal is that the amount of time and risk associated with recovering the substation would be a waste of resources that could better be spent elsewhere. Simply put, punishing you is not as important as recovering the substation. That works more to your benefit than ours."

Boaz sighed. "I'm not saying I stole it, but . . . I may know where it is."

"I suspect you do."

"It'll be back in place in a few days."

Railas turned to Halloran. "Does the plaintiff wish to make any further conditions?"

Halloran shook his head. Railas could see betrayed looks on some of the spectators, particularly the other outsiders. A line had been drawn in the sand, and they didn't like it.

"Then I consider this matter concluded," Railas announced, "pending confirmation that the existing conditions are met."

And then, recognizing a frantic gesture from Amy, Railas retrieved the plastic gavel and gently tapped it on the desk. The courtroom began to clear.

As Railas gathered his accessories and put them into his case, he couldn't help but notice the self-congratulating looks on both Halloran's and Rittenhouse's faces. Miller didn't seem particularly impressed either way and the bailiff was out the door before Railas could gauge his reaction. Clearly those most directly involved in establishing his role here were pleased with his first challenge. Halloran himself walked over, his large form actually dwarfing Railas's at close range.

"Good work," he said, offering Railas his hand.

"There's no need to thank me," Railas said, "though

it's obvious that the case proceeded in an advantageous manner for you."

He shrugged. "I don't mind giving the little rat a break as long as he leaves our stuff alone."

"But there is the matter of his other crimes," Railas pointed out.

"What other crimes?" Halloran asked, genuinely surprised.

"As I mentioned, some of his commercial exploits are suspect. This could suggest black marketeering, possible extortion, and various vice charges."

Halloran waved his hand. "That's not important."

"Actually, it is, Mr. Halloran, and that's the point. In the position you've assigned me I must investigate crime where I see it, and I must do so impartially. Even if no direct complaint is filed, it's possible this may be part of a larger picture."

Halloran looked hesitant. "Don't worry about the larger picture. We'll take care of that . . . In time."

And, though Railas hadn't suggested how he might proceed, he couldn't help but notice concern in Halloran's face. Concern and something else . . . He studied the documents he had collected. There was more here, whether the humans could see it or not. But they *could* see it, that much he was sure of. The data was in no way hidden. The real question was, did they want to?

Chapter Nine
Downstairs

The security office was a non-descript window in the shopping mall of the common area, and it was not particularly fortified. Railas had seen the orange-suited deputies among the people, but they didn't stand out. He still assumed they were armed, but didn't know the details. Only one man occupied the office, the same person he'd seen in the court room. He sat behind a console, keeping track of multiple screens of data. Railas easily interfaced with the display, recognizing its content as general information concerning the local goings-on. It included the output of all security cameras as well as the schedule of industrial traffic. He also seemed to be monitoring shift changes and bank activity. His fingers tapped the console in a mock drumbeat while he surveyed the data, as if he were playing some version of air guitar. What he didn't seem to be aware of was what was happening directly in front of him.

"Officer Gibbs," Railas said.

The man was startled briefly, and appeared genuinely

surprised to see Railas. Surprised and concerned. Like many he'd seen here, Gibbs was youngish, but aside from the uniform he didn't look the part of a security officer. His upper body was not particularly developed and his overall demeanor suggested a high-strung temperament, lacking confidence. His orange hair flew in wisps as he regained his composure.

"Railas," he acknowledged. "The robot guy. Okay . . . what's up? What are you doing here?"

"I'm here concerning an investigation," he replied. "May I ask you some questions?"

Gibbs looked confused. "What investigation?"

"The matter of Harmy Boaz."

He stammered, as if caught off guard. "But . . . That case is closed, isn't it? There was a deal . . ."

"Yes, I know," Railas agreed. "I was there."

"So . . . What's the issue?"

"This is a follow-up investigation."

"Oh . . ." Gibbs eyed him suspiciously. "I wasn't aware there was anything to follow up on. We'll be monitoring the return of the substation. We'll let you know if there are any developments."

"I'm following up on some issues that arose from the case," Railas explained. "I'd prefer not to close the file until I've at least made note of them. I thought your office might be able to clear up a few matters."

He shrugged. "Okay, shoot. How can I help you?"

"First of all, I suppose you could say I'm new here, and I'm not quite sure what jurisdiction your office falls into. Can I assume you function as sheriff or some such thing?"

Gibbs thought for a moment, as if unsure himself. "We manage the place, provide a police presence, keep order," he said with a shrug. "I suppose we do function as the sheriff's department or at least routine security. We're not that big out here more or less . . ."

"And you handle arrests and confinement?"

He chuckled. "Confinement? We don't do much of that, but . . . yeah it comes up. Got a few interview rooms back there, and one or two detention rooms." He nodded to the doorway behind him. "You've got to understand, we're all basically confined here no matter what, so . . ."

Railas nodded. "I'm hearing that a lot. Nonetheless, we're talking about criminal segregation and the punishment of crime."

"Oh, Halloran takes care of that mostly."

"How? Are you saying he manages other jail facilities?"

He shook his head. "No, you're getting this all wrong. If our people get out of line he talks to them. Sometimes he pulls contracts or gives them punishment duty, but jail . . . That just doesn't happen."

"What about in the case of violent crime or theft?"

He shrugged. "Maybe you should talk to Mr. Halloran about that."

"But it was my understanding that my appointment was supposed to mark the end of that general attitude," Railas said. "Which is one of the reasons Mr. Boaz was so upset–"

"Oh, don't worry about Hell Diver," he laughed. "No, we didn't tell him, but that was part of the fun!"

"Fun?"

"Yeah, he came to deal. Halloran wanted to see how he'd react –"

"Yes, he wanted to see his face," Railas interrupted. "Maybe that begins to answer my question. You're saying that nothing much is expected to change."

Gibbs straightened up slightly, as if uncomfortable. "Oh, don't get me wrong. Halloran wants you here, so do I. But the actual dealing . . . well, most of that's pretty standard . . . Is Rittenhouse . . . Did you talk to *him* about this?"

"I could, but right now I'm asking you."

Gibbs looked annoyed. "Look, most of what I do is monitor stuff, keep track of what's going on, and make sure things are under control." He tapped his display. "It's not that hard a job. I really just hang out in here –"

"I can see that," Railas agreed, gesturing to the console. "And I realize there's a difference between law enforcement here and on Earth. But you must have occasional violent crime. Surely those sorts of things would be handled differently."

Gibbs snorted. "Oooh, yeah, that doesn't happen very often. Halloran takes a hard view of things like that. Not good for business. Not inside, anyway."

"Then I'm to understand you ship such people to other jurisdictions."

"Doesn't need to happen, but yeah, you could call it that . . ."

Gibbs' flicker of a grin was brief enough that Railas almost missed it. Something in his pattern-matching system found this to be significant, but he wasn't sure why.

Gibbs sighed and shook his head. "You got to understand, Halloran has people who deal with stuff like that before it happens."

"Like what happened to Mindy?"

His face dropped. "Who told you about that?"

"I'm told her situation was settled outside the law, more or less . . ."

Gibbs' face puckered into something between annoyance and concern. "Are you sure you don't want to talk to Rittenhouse about this? You know you really don't have to get involved with that side of –"

"What about the money in Boaz's account?"

Gibbs sighed and looked away, as if hoping Railas would simply disappear. "Look, that has nothing to do with his case. It wasn't about money, it was a missing substation. I know Halloran told you that much at least! The guy gets around, that's all. He's an outsider. Some of them do rather well, or they get lucky. It's not really our business where the money comes from."

"Normally, no," Railas agreed. "But we're not talking about regular commerce. Here money is different. Most of it is circulated in a closed system. A zero-sum game. Some people profit from the losses of others."

Gibbs' jaw dropped. "Look, now you're getting into a can of worms you really don't need to open. People have money, people spend it. Not our business. That goes *way* beyond what Halloran needed you for, and Rittenhouse –"

"My job description is quite clear in this regard,"

Railas interrupted. "And Dr. Rittenhouse *did* intend for me to function as an investigator. I'm not law enforcement, I don't make arrests, but I'm at least supposed to be curious."

Gibbs smiled again, this time with a kind of wonder. "Yeah . . . I guess so. You know, I just didn't think you'd come around and ask about that sort of stuff." He shrugged. "Well, okay, let me give you the lay of the land." He indicated the console. "You look at the layout here and you can see the stuff that matters. That's me. We police, we manage, we make sure the lights are on. Halloran wants everything clean and polished, you know."

"Of course. Just how clean is it?"

"Very," Gibbs assured him. "But the dirt has to go somewhere, right? Most of it goes outside. People like Boaz are like alley cats. No table manners. We've got investors to think about, hotels and hospitality. Nobody wants to see the outsiders, at least not up close. I mean, we *see* them, but when they're in here they have to behave. Guild rules."

"Guild," Railas commented.

"Boaz, not so much, but the refinery workers answer to the guild. Code of conduct, that sort of thing. You cross the guild, that's grounds for contract issues. Also, you got to understand, people who do that sort of work play rough sometimes, rougher than we like. The guild provides supervision there. Some of those guys are pretty tough."

"Wait a minute," Railas stopped him. "Are you describing a kind of criminal family?"

"Not criminal," Gibbs insisted with a thoughtful pause. "But it *is* a family. And some of the daddies have to give a few spankings now and then."

Railas nodded. "I see why you don't use your detention cells."

"Now, the money . . ." He looked pained. "Not sure how to put this . . ."

"Boaz's money," Railas said.

"Well, there's inside, there's outside and then there's . . . downstairs."

"Downstairs," Railas repeated.

"These are honest people here, most of them don't mean anybody any harm, right?"

"Of course."

"But they are *people*," Gibbs emphasized. "Stuff that happens downstairs is stuff we don't *want* to know about."

"Vice," Railas suggested.

"Boaz gets lucky with the cards sometimes.

Sometimes not."

"Gambling."

"Not our proudest moment, but as long as it's not up here . . . It happens downstairs."

"In the Sandbox, perhaps?" Railas asked.

Gibbs almost jumped. "What? Who told you about that?"

"It's listed on your display," Railas said. "I'm seeing regular activity from that location, more so than in the common area. What is this sandbox?"

"Uhm . . . Well, it's nothing. Nothing you need to concern yourself with . . ."

"Is it downstairs? I mean literally, is it in the lower levels?"

Gibbs thought for a moment and nodded. "Yeah, very much downstairs. It's kind of a night club, if such a thing can exist here. Look, just don't go there, okay? I shouldn't even be talking about it –"

"They gamble in the Sandbox?"

Gibbs nodded. But then he paused again, gathering his thoughts. "You know who uses sandboxes? Cats do."

"Interesting metaphor."

"You know what cat's do in sandboxes?"

"I assume you mean pet cats."

"Yeah. Well, that's where they go to do stuff you don't want them doing anywhere else. Same thing here. You see somebody here, insider, outsider, whatever, and they do what they're supposed to be doing. Now, that very same person goes into the sandbox and . . . well, they may do something they have to do, for whatever reason, but *can't* do up here. Now, people like Mindy may have issues, too. I don't know how much you know about her, but let's just say she had some supplemental income. She kind of worked two jobs here. And, when you do that . . . Well, sometimes you bring work home with you."

Railas nodded. "If I'm interpreting your words properly, you appear to be telling me that Mindy began her association with . . . Wedge in the Sandbox. Prostitution?"

"Not always. Now, that *is* illegal. But dancing, escorting, stuff like that . . . Well, that's how money goes from one account into another around here. Fair enough? Do I have to say more? The Sandbox is not our business. It's not part of what we do. That's why. Now, can we leave it at that?"

"Possibly," Railas said. "But that depends on how far it goes. You see, even that doesn't explain where Boaz gets his money from, or his reputation. People are afraid of him. I saw that. What else happens in the Sandbox?"

Gibbs shook his head. "I'm paid *not to* know. C'mon, Railas, give these people their privacy. Don't go digging around in peoples' —"

"I take it you don't go down there, wherever it is, do you?"

"Not generally," he admitted.

"Or at least not when you're wearing that orange uniform."

Gibbs' lack of response said volumes.

Railas turned to leave and Gibbs let out a quiet sigh of relief and sat more comfortably in his chair, though he didn't immediately go back to his mindless drumming. Railas scanned his records regarding the layout of the complex, focusing on the lower levels where the yellow room was. What was downstairs that was so worth hiding?

Chapter Ten
Sandbox

The elevator to the lower levels was remarkably slow, and for no real reason that Railas could imagine, just as the one to the governor's office had been. Since there were few levels in total, this did not present a problem, but it was annoying, particularly to a being capable of thinking several times faster than a human. Thankfully there was no elevator music. The lower most level of Shangri-La was where the yellow room had been, though Railas had lost track of where it actually was, and, since it had no significance other than being the room he first emerged from, he saw no reason to use it as a frame of reference. But, were he to guess, he'd suspect that the place he was looking for would be as far away from the yellow room as possible.

Where does one hide something on such a small world as Shangri-La? He consulted the diagrams of the lower level, which looked much like a circular labyrinth, weaving in and around the support structure for the colony. He assumed his destination would be nowhere

near a common thoroughfare, which ruled out any transfer
tunnels leading to the methane refining and storage
facilities or other important industrial zones. Similarly, he
could rule out food and water production and other
infrastructure that would need to be available for
inspection. That left only a few obvious choices. The
most logical place was a region simply marked "general
storage." Also, since there was a maintenance note
describing the space as 'unfinished,' the schematics had no
final specifications for size or configuration. Railas set off
in the direction of this area, his legs reluctantly adjusting
to the strange gravity of the seemingly sticky floor. As he
approached the section he saw evidence of far more traffic
along the path than would be expected for a supposedly
empty storage room. As he drew nearer he could detect a
combination of musical tones and conversation. A
partition with a plastic curtain served as the official
boundary. Above were the words "Sandbox."

Once beyond the curtain the sound of chaos grew
louder. Railas had imagined a few scenarios that might
present themselves. So far, what he saw met his
expectations. Beyond the first partition was a length of
empty corridor leading to another curtain, further buffering
the sound. Waiting at the second door was a man dressed

similarly to Boaz, minus the armor. His attire could have been assembled from many uniforms, but was not a uniform in itself. His worn pants were patched with various colors of cloth and his jacket was stitched together from garments of roughly similar size. He'd noticed other outsiders dressed in this fashion. One could assume that, since most textiles could only originate from Earth, clothing not provided by the colony would be expensive. But, as pathetic as this might look in another context, the posture of the man did not indicate destitution or low status. Far from it. It could also be that his clothing was literally assembled from trophies acquired from rivals. Railas still had much to learn about the residents inside and outside Shangri-La, and he was surprised at how much was not documented, or apparently not admitted to. Like the other outsiders, this man did not look particularly strong, but his features made him appear hardened, having much in common with known criminals in his database. Clearly his creators intended Railas to be a good judge of character.

The man looked surprised to see Railas, and possibly alarmed. But there was something else in his expression that didn't add up. Railas might expect a man with something to hide to be alarmed at the presence of authority, but in this case he seemed more annoyed than frightened, as if Railas represented an unwelcome change in his routine rather than a genuine threat. There was also confusion. Railas was not only *not* on whatever guest list the man was checking, but he was outside the boundaries of that list altogether, and not even in the same volume. He could learn nothing from this reaction in itself, but he filed it away for future reference.

The man looked him up and down, making a point of blocking his path. "You're him, ain't you? The robot guy, right?"

"I'm Railas, from the judicial court," he announced. "And I suppose it would be accurate to call me a robot, as opposed to an android."

The man looked confused, backing up to continue blocking his path. "So . . . Are you lost?"

"No," Railas assured him. "Though I assume you deliberately made this place hard to find."

"Look, I . . . Well, maybe you should talk to Halloran or . . ."

"Rittenhouse," he finished for him.

"Yeah, that guy. Look, you really shouldn't . . . Why are you here?"

"I'm conducting an investigation," Railas said.

"In *there?*" he said, as if the idea was unthinkable.

"Yes."

"Uhm . . ."

"Since you mentioned Halloran and Rittenhouse, they gave me direct access to all areas of this installation as part of my function."

"Well, but . . . Perhaps you could give us some advance notice or–"

"I'm not inspecting your gathering place, I'm simply collecting information."

The man looked uncertain, but finally stepped aside. He did, however, reach for some kind of covert communication device, probably to alert others that an agent of the law was approaching. Railas wondered if it would have been possible for him to disguise himself had he wanted to.

The cavern was larger than the schematics indicated, and was the first crowded room Railas had seen. Again, no uniforms, and the clothing he saw looked frayed and in some cases miss-sized. The music came from a cheap sound system, authentic Earth design, and possibly jerry rigged to work with the more sophisticated tablet controls the operator used. Railas had no framework to identify the music being played, but it did not appear to be the main event. All attention was directed at three women dancing on a platform. These were better dressed than the others, but their clothing was by its nature more sparse. Railas could only assume this was part of the vice he'd expected to see. Other groups of humans sat around tables playing what appeared to be games of chance. Some held datapads that simulated hands of cards. Other scantily dressed women circulated the room with what Railas assumed to be refreshment.

Railas first approached a table where three men and two women were playing a dice game. As he got closer, one of them jumped with surprise. But then he laughed.

"Hey, look at this!" he shouted. "Cool! He's here!" And then the others laughed as well, not appearing at all afraid of Railas. In fact, they seemed to be suggesting that he join them. They all had tentative smiles, as if expecting his presence to be part of some kind of joke. But they did leave room for him to sit.

Railas took up the same posture that they did, trying to navigate the bench in human fashion. In the hollow of the table was a single die that appeared to be the focus of the game. It was hollow, with another smaller die within. Railas was not familiar with the game, but he didn't have to be in order to participate.

"Care to match?" one of them asked, a dark man with Asian features. Out of respect, Railas did not try to determine his name. "One role each, cool color," he announced. "Fifty bits to open."

"And you bet on the results?" Railas asked them.

"Simple game," a bald man with a goatee said.

"How high are the stakes typically?"

All shrugged.

"Do any of you play with a man named Harmy Boaz? He is otherwise known as 'Hell Diver.'"

Their faces dropped. "Seriously . . . ?" an older woman with silver braided hair regarded him, no longer amused. "You're looking for Hell Diver in here? The actual Hell Diver?"

Railas nodded. "Does he come here?"

The others at the table exchanged glances. "We don't know Hell Diver," the man with the goatee said. "We just come here to play . . ."

"This is supposed to be the sandbox," the dark man spoke up. "We're not actually part of . . . I mean, we have nothing to do with . . . We thought you were . . ."

"What?" Railas asked, genuinely confused. Now all their faces took on fear. What was going on here?

"House rules," a voice spoke from behind.

Railas turned to see another, more official-looking man hovering over him. He wore a suit rather than a uniform, and, like the attire of the women, it was slightly higher in quality than would normally be available.

"If you're not playing, you don't sit," he scolded. "Looks like you need to be in for fifty bits. If not, don't slow the roll."

Railas stood.

In the room lighting it would actually be harder than usual to ID the man, but Railas saw no need. The fact that he was there confirmed his suspicions.

"Can we help you?" He asked Railas.

"I'm looking for associates of Hell Diver."

He shook his head. "You won't find them here. You've got this place all wrong."

Railas made a point of scanning the room.

"Off duty people come down here to take a deep breath. To get *off stage*, so to speak."

Railas glanced at the other gamblers at the table. None had attempted to resume the game. They seemed enthralled in the conversation, as if they were watching a drama of some kind.

"You want to get away from the rules," Railas said to the man in the suit.

"That's right. We want to have somewhere to go where we don't have to sing and dance with Mr. Halloran."

"Downstairs," Railas confirmed.

"Yeah, and we like to keep it to ourselves. A little fun, which you might not care to understand, but we do. You don't have jurisdiction here," he emphasized. "You're not supposed to *be* here."

Railas considered. "Well, as I *am* here, how am I a threat to you?"

"You make people nervous," he grumbled. "Don't interrupt the games if you don't want to play. You don't eat, obviously, and I doubt you came to enjoy the music or . . . other entertainment."

"I don't have arrest powers," he promised.

The man, who was clearly a type of bouncer, looked at him long and hard. "Okay, we'll play along. After all, we've got nothing to hide here." And then he walked away, as if he had somewhere else to go, whether he did or not. Railas assumed he'd be taking the next step and contacting Rittenhouse or Halloran, neither of which knew he was there. He had only moments to gather his information and he couldn't be sure of another opportunity. He'd also become aware of some of the other activity in the room, a thing alluded to earlier, but never stated directly. The women dancing were not the only females there. Some congregated near a passage leading elsewhere. Based on his understanding of vice, this likely meant a more discrete and private sort of entertainment, and possibly another angle to explore. In the crowded room even Railas's form could be hard to distinguish from that of others, though his metallic head resembled a helmet and his bare shoulders contained exposed panels that were not human-like. Fortunately, the other humans were distracted with their own pursuits and his presence was not yet drawing attention. If he sauntered closer to the edge of the room, the crowd itself could hide him. On his journey he catalogued more vices. The drinks being served were highly alcoholic, which he could tell by sampling the air. The crowd was also cover for covert exchanges of what were likely controlled substances. This was the part of Shangri-La that Halloran wanted to keep secret. A contrast to his clean and orderly world above.

The women reacted to him in a similar fashion as the table of gamblers had. But some of these faces were familiar. He had not categorized every face in the colony, but he'd seen these people upstairs. Apparently, this was the double life that many of the workers lived. Like the dancers, their clothing was intended to display their bodily characteristics, thus it did not need to be substantial. As a group they appeared annoyed more than afraid, again Railas couldn't interpret why.

"May I speak to you?" he asked.

"We're busy," a dark haired woman said. "And we've got nothing to say."

"I'm not judging you," he assured her. "I'm seeking information on another matter."

"We're on the clock," the woman said, flinging her hair back. "Talking costs money."

"I have money," Railas said, suddenly realizing it himself. "Technically, I'm employed by the station and I do draw a paycheck. I have an advance to cover expenses."

The woman smiled a strange smile. "This could be interesting," she admitted. "Two hundred bits buys for an hour . . . with restrictions, of course."

Railas shook his head. "I'm not permitted to participate in vice, which I suspect that would qualify as. I also cannot give the appearance of committing an impropriety. I can, however, offer a general gratuity of no more than twenty bits . . . for appreciation of service employees."

"Twenty for six minutes?" She chuckled. "How

about we make it an even ten? "But I don't guarantee I can answer anything," she warned. "I'll listen and talk, that's it. Hypothetical conversation."

The others looked suspicious. A red haired woman shook her head. "He's not supposed to be down here. Something's wrong . . ."

"You think she can't earn more than twenty bits in ten minutes?" a dark skinned woman with blue hair challenged. "Maybe you can throw in something to trade." She gently touched the metal in his elbow joint. And, if Railas could truly feel fear, he might have considered this a threat.

"We need to do this now," the dark haired woman said. "I'm game." She took his hand, as if savoring an unusual experience. "Call me Fire Swirl.'"

Railas identified the woman as Shelley McClusky by her face print, or a still image he'd caught of it in the strobe lighting. She had no official criminal record, suggesting that the lifestyle she took on downstairs was new to her, though she was good at presenting the illusion that she'd done it for years. She led him to a secluded room with little furniture, but a substantial enough door to provide significant sound dampening.

"Fire Swirl," she repeated. "You sure you don't want to try . . . I mean, it'd probably be a first! But, hey, the clock starts now, get busy."

"I'm to understand that you humans down here are trading with each other."

"That's one way to put it."

"And the company does not support nor stop this."

She chuckled. "That's complicated."

"I need to know if there are other revenue streams, larger ones that could account for greater sums of money in circulation. More than could be accounted for in trade."

She looked confused. "Just how much money are you talking about?"

"Close to ten million bits."

She straightened up. "*Nobody* has *that* kind of money! But, if they do, we don't ask about it."

"Where does the money come from, hypothetically?"

"Trade," she said. "Losers spend their paychecks to have fun. People like me try to earn enough to break contract . . . Other than that . . ."

"Other than that . . . ?"

"Outsiders," she said with a shrug. "They have money, sometimes more than they should." She sighed. "That's probably what you're looking for. But millions?"

She shook her head.

"Where does it come from?" Railas prodded. "Where do the outsiders get their money?"

"Where do you think?" she laughed. "Off station, off books. Stuff you can't get even here." She motioned around the room.

"And what did Boaz . . . Hell Diver do to get it? What do you know about him?"

She shook her head, her face taking on a look between fear and disgust. "He has particular tastes. *Expensive* tastes," she said more quietly. "What he wants can't happen here. He needs micro-gravity . . . Is this off the record? Look, the guilds look out for each other, even the outsiders . . . I can't be mixed up in–"

"I'm asking in confidence. It shouldn't even be necessary to identify you as a source."

She laughed. "You had him on trial. You made a deal just like always. Nothing different."

"This may be."

She paused, looking him over and taking a deep breath. "He took me to a party once . . . outside."

"Outside the station?"

"Out there, yes. He flew me in his rig. He had a place . . ." She stopped, swallowed hard and looked directly into his camera eyes. The effect was strange. Something about her doing this made a connection. She was searching for something, something a robot shouldn't have. Did he have this, whatever it is that makes a person trust?

"Did he harm you?" Railas asked.

"No, not me, but I wasn't the only one there. I saw folks who supposedly . . . who'd left . . ."

"What people?"

"Look, I saw people there off contract. Some who . . ."

"Are you saying you saw people who were missing? People who weren't supposed to still be on the planet?"

"Yeah, some. I think. Off contract people . . ."

"People who couldn't afford transport to Earth?"

She nodded. "And some others. People we didn't know where they went. He partied with them. Plenty of pills to go around and . . . oils and stuff."

"Are you saying these women were intoxicated?"

"Not like they didn't want it, but . . ."

"You didn't."

She shook her head. "Neither did the girl who came with me. We left . . ."

"Was Mindy there?"

Her eyes grew sharper. "Look, Mindy created her own problems! She knew what she was getting into!"

"Was she there?"

She nodded. "Once."

"So, you've been there on more than one occasion. Could you describe the room? Where was it?"

She shook her head. "It all looks the same out there, except . . ."

"What?"

"I saw a lake, a big one . . ."

"What did the room look like? What were its dimensions?" Railas asked.

"Small, . . . long, . . . just a box."

"A rectangular room or suite of rooms? Like a dormitory? Only one entrance?"

She nodded, looking concerned at his recognition.

"Was the ceiling higher than eight feet?"

She shook her head.

"Could this have been the interior of a methane substation?"

Her eyes lit up briefly, the idea taking hold.

"Is it possible that Hell Diver uses stolen facilities for this elicit . . . behavior? Did you see anybody else there? A client you wouldn't recognize from Shangri-La?"

But then the door swung open and the well-dressed guard marched in. Railas now identified him as Nathanial Woods, a supervisor in the methane refinery, apparently moonlighting as the Sandbox's bouncer and . . . dealer.

"We sell hours, not minutes!" he shouted. "You don't get to peel one banana off the bunch. But your ten minutes are up anyway, robot! This is the kind of interference we don't want!"

"I'm interested in crimes going on outside, not down here," he assured him.

"You don't listen, do you?" he growled. "Hell Diver ain't here! But, guess what! I am!" And then he swung, his arm only slightly encumbered by his suit jacket. For a resident, his upper body strength was more formidable than Boaz's was likely to be. The blow actually shifted Railas, seeing as his feet, equipped with magnetic locks, had no metal to take hold of. But he was able to adjust his position to absorb the blow and take advantage of the higher gravity on the ground. The man's fist clunked on the lower part of his face, the angular edges of his chassis cutting into his knuckles.

His scream was silent as he drew back his hand, doing a pantomime dance of pain that might have been comical in other circumstances.

"My hardware is that of a Robo-Naut, a unit designed to operate in space," Railas boasted. "This body is rated to take a direct hit from a baseball-sized meteor, not unlike a nineteenth century cannon ball, and still remain operational. Your hand is basically made out of water and hamburger. You've just punched a piece of industrial machinery."

"You damned . . ."

"The good news, of course, is that I doubt even *I* could make a case for assault, seeing as I'm a non-human. The bad news is, I suspect your hand will be useless to you for at least a day and may require minor surgery."

And then another form appeared in the doorway. It was Rittenhouse, his shirt only partially buttoned. "Railas, what the hell are you doing?"

"I was following a lead," he said.

"For what?" he demanded, evidently out of breath. "You don't have a case yet!"

"I was not satisfied with some of the details concerning Boaz."

"Look, this isn't your jurisdiction!" he shouted. "This is *downstairs!* Even *I'm* not supposed to be here!"

"I believe there may be more to this place than simple vice–"

"Look, you've got to tell me if you want to come down here. This is *way* out of bounds for this project!" He took his hand. "Please, let's get you out of here before you make things worse!"

Railas regarded the wounded man. He then turned to the woman called Fire Swirl. Neither looked him in the eye. And then he allowed Rittenhouse to guide him out into the quieter world outside.

Chapter Eleven
The Yellow Room

"What the hell is wrong with you?" Rittenhouse
demanded.

Railas's initial assumption had been right. The
journey to the yellow room had been a roughly straight
line from the Sandbox, and he was quite certain it was on
the opposite side of the installation. He was unsure why
Rittenhouse chose this room as a default meeting place,
but it did not surprise him. Both chairs remained in the
room, but neither of them chose to sit down. Rittenhouse
paced back and forth, alternating between being speechless
and too emotional to get words out.

"What were you thinking?" he demanded. "How did
you even get in there?"

When Rittenhouse finally faced him expecting an
answer, Railas wasn't sure where to begin. "I was
conducting an investigation," he repeated.

"What investigation?" he shouted. "The Boaz matter
was settled and there's nothing even on the docket until
next week!"

111

"The Boaz matter itself was settled, but it opened up other questions."

"And that led you to the Sandbox?" he said, still unsure if he could believe his own words.

"Yes, I was following a lead."

"A lead? What are you, a detective now?" he laughed, dancing in frustration.

"No, not a detective nor a police officer. I don't claim to have arrest powers. But I did not get a satisfactory answer to my inquiries from station law enforcement. Under such circumstances, my office becomes ultimately responsible for gathering and preserving evidence of crime."

Rittenhouse's jaw dropped, making him look more shaken than Railas could have imagined seeing him. "Really? You came up with this all by yourself?" His grin tried to return. "Wow, nobody could have predicted that! But . . . The Sandbox? You got all the way *downstairs?*"

"I fail to see why that comes as such a surprise," Railas admitted. "In any case, you may not be aware of the magnitude of what I've discovered so far. Boaz is an incredibly dangerous man and he may be guilty of capital crimes –"

"Boaz?" he shouted, pacing again. "Capital crimes?

The man's a sniveling nuisance, guilty of nothing but mischief –"

"Possible human trafficking and abuse are not mischief," Railas insisted, raising his voice for emphasis. "I'm also concerned that this substation may be involved in something far more serious than methane misappropriation. We may even have a case for piracy."

"You spoke to . . ."

"Shelley McClusky, yes. And she could well be a valuable witness –"

"You *believed* what she said?" He gasped. "Just like that?"

Railas paused. "I see no reason why she would lie."

"She's a bit player who wants attention! She was making up stories, for heaven's sake!" He laughed. "What the heck did she even tell you?"

"She is a witness to clandestine gatherings involving mostly women, at least some of which were kept intoxicated, possibly against their will –"

"That's crazy!"

"Nonetheless, an investigation must be conducted," Railas insisted. "We must find the substation and search it before Boaz has a chance to destroy any evidence. I also recommend that Boaz himself be held in custody."

"Custody?" Rittenhouse stood in awe, his eyes wide and his head slowly shaking back and forth. "You're saying we make an arrest? We hold him at the station? Hell Diver?"

Railas nodded. "He is both a criminal and a material witness. He must be questioned under oath and his story verified. Obviously he and his associates have eluded station security before, which does not surprise me. I don't want to speak ill of your personnel here, but Officer Gibbs doesn't seem at all interested in pursuing or punishing crime, and I would go so far as to say that he is actively ignoring evidence of it. Station security seems to be a police force in name only. The question now is whether or not the governor was aware of any of this. If not, it's my job to inform him."

"Just who do you think this guy is?" Rittenhouse demanded, finally stopping and facing him.

"Somebody who's managed to amass far more money than would be possible for this . . . limited nuisance you described."

"Money? What money?"

"Harmy Boaz's financial records show an enormous influx of funds that cannot be accounted for –"

"What? Nonsense! How much money are we even

talking about?"

"Almost ten million bits –"

"Ten million? That's insane!"

"Nonetheless, it's true."

Rittenhouse's jaw dropped again. "And you accessed his financial records as part of your assessment of his case?"

Railas nodded.

"Well, that's simply impossible, I can assure you," he said, shaking his head. He then reached into the drawer of the table and withdrew a tablet, punching in some quick commands. He then glanced up at Railas. "Can you give me access to that data?"

Railas tapped the pad with his finger and a spreadsheet emerged.

"You've got to be kidding me!" he said, looking over the figures. He fingered the sheet up and down several times, shaking his head in disbelief.

"You see the funds," Railas confirmed. "At this moment they total nine million, five hundred and seventy five thousand bits, pending two transfers. And that's *after* he paid his court costs to Mr. Halloran."

Rittenhouse shook the pad between his fingers. "This is not right," he insisted. "Where did this . . ." Then he laughed. "Oh, I see." He tapped the tablet. "That's a math error! A misplaced decimal point!"

Railas shook his head. "This data comes directly from the colony network, updated several times. If the Earth-based banking system made an error this large, they surely would have cleared it up by now. This is not a data-entry error made by some administrator in the office upstairs. The money is real enough. The question is where he got it."

"But . . ." He sighed and finally nodded. "Okay, so from this you deduce what exactly?"

"McClusky described what could be human trafficking and piracy. She also spoke of 'off station' and 'off books' money, which could suggest illegal trade with outside entities, perhaps other colonies or even wealthy rogues engaging in crimes. I'm told that outsiders come and go, and that such people may die or 'disappear' from time to time. We may be dealing with organized crime above and beyond the governor's office. Or maybe starting with it."

Rittenhouse gasped. "Amazing!" he whispered. "Completely amazing!" His smile returned. "You know, you weren't expected to do anything like this! But, seriously, this changes everything . . ."

"Dr. Rittenhouse, as much as I understand your interest in this project, we are now talking about bigger things than whether or not I'm performing as expected, or even if this whole idea makes sense. I believe you may have humans in danger as we speak, particularly people like Mindy."

"Mindy?" Rittenhouse asked, his expression quizzical.

"I suspect McClusky did see her when she became involved with Boaz at his 'party' as she called it, and she does fit the pattern –"

"Look, forget Mindy, she's . . ."

"What?"

"Do you intend to interview her? Do you intend to interview Mindy?"

"Of course."

He began to pace again, nodding his head and whispering to himself. "So, what is it you intend to do? I mean about the substation. I'm curious."

Railas nodded. "As I said during the hearing, we have the approximate position of where it must be. I suggest we enter it and search for signs of the missing people as well as other possible crimes."

"Wait a minute . . . Did you say 'we?' You're

planning to go out there yourself?"

"Of course."

"But that's . . . completely out of the question! You're talking about going outside. *Outside!*" he repeated.

"Yes."

"You can't survive out there!"

"Neither can you," he countered.

"But you couldn't even *walk* out there," he scoffed. "Your magnetic shoes won't work, and the slightest breeze would blow you over!"

"That is also true of you," he pressed. "And, though I don't breathe or require air pressure, I'm aware that the seals in my chassis that protect my critical systems are not rated for that kind of environment. Neither are my joints and servos. The liquefied gasses could be expected to cause damage, possibly serious damage."

Rittenhouse nodded.

"Therefore, rather than walking the route, I will need access to a vehicle. A 'rig' I've heard them called. Surely you can arrange this."

Rittenhouse whistled. "Wow! Seriously? You'd be willing to risk that?"

"Yes."

He ran his fingers through his hair and paced again.

"This is an interesting development."

"But you do appear to see my point. If Boaz is collecting humans for nefarious purposes, they could be in jeopardy right now," Railas warned. "Knowing this, I must take any action necessary to resolve the situation or I become equally guilty. Can we assume that my training is complete? Can we stop testing and verifying my functions and simply work on getting those women safely back to the station?"

Rittenhouse shrugged. "You've got a point," he admitted. "But, yeah, we're past training, way past! We've just thrown away *that* book altogether!"

Chapter Twelve
Story Lines

The elevator ride to Halloran's office was slow, as usual, more so with the tension between Railas and Rittenhouse. And what awaited them at the top was no better.

Halloran wasn't at his desk this time, which Railas noted as significant. His practiced composure was all but broken now, as his formerly organized world was clearly in damage control mode. His jacket was open and he dabbed at his head with a handkerchief. Even in one of the coldest known worlds, the man had managed to break a sweat. His face was particularly sour and his eyes more wide-open than usual. He stood at the window overlooking the complex, his hand having left a print on the glass where he'd been leaning against it. Commiserating with him was the orange-suited security officer, Gibbs. His face reflected the pain of a brutal tongue lashing, and Railas suspected he and Rittenhouse would be next.

"Where the hell do you get off?" he demanded,

directing his gaze to Railas. "The Sandbox? Really? Where did you get the idea you could even *consider* doing something like this?"

"Part of my instatement here involved having access to station. I don't recall any specific areas being restricted."

"That's because you weren't supposed to know it *existed!*"

"And why is that?"

"Well . . ." Halloran wagged his finger, trying to come up with words that weren't there.

"The Sandbox is outside your jurisdiction," Rittenhouse said for him. "You're employed here to handle official station business. That's supposed to be restricted to matters that come before the court."

"Yes, and it was in connection with one of those cases that I expanded my investigation there."

"I never told you to do that!" Gibbs spoke up.

"Yes you did!" Halloran turned on him. "You said the word Sandbox! That's literally the dumbest thing you could have done!"

"No, *he* said that! He read it off my status display!"

"Same thing!"

"And it's not like I told him where it was!" Gibbs

defended." I didn't even think he could find it!"

"Yes, I think we all underestimated his resourcefulness," Rittenhouse agreed, trying to calm the mood. "But the existence of the Sandbox isn't the issue. Of course, as official station personnel, he doesn't have jurisdiction there –"

"Yes he does," Railas interrupted. "The very purpose of my office is to serve the interests of justice. I'm also supposed to be impartial in that everyone, including those in this room, must recognize my rulings. And, odd as it may seem, the mere presence of that establishment is not a crime. My concerns now are for *genuine* crimes, things that go beyond even the understood 'arrangements' you seem to have."

"What the hell is he talking about?" Halloran asked Rittenhouse.

"He's talking about human trafficking, possible forced prostitution, kidnapping, and worse," Railas answered for him.

At this, Halloran froze in mid movement and stared. "What? . . . Where's he getting that crap from?"

"From direct interrogation of witnesses," Railas answered.

"McClusky was telling stories," Rittenhouse said with

122

a sigh.

"Who?"

"Shelley McClusky –"

"Who the hell's that?"

"She works in the personnel office –"

"With a station this small, you're telling me you don't know all your employees?" Railas asked Halloran. "Or do you know her more properly as Fire Swirl?"

Halloran gasped, stepped closer to Railas, and he may well have considered striking him. Then he took a deep breath. "McClusky," he whispered. "Personnel . . . Yes, of course, Shelley. . . . New kid . . ."

"She probably misunderstood what Railas was asking her," Rittenhouse suggested. "Either that or she was in a particularly creative mood. She told him quite a yarn."

"Her testimony and her answers to my questions did not seem dishonest or fictional," Railas said. "Like any witness, she offered only one point of view, but it will be taken into account as I continue my investigation–"

"Continue?" Halloran demanded.

Rittenhouse sighed. "Under the circumstances, however McClusky came up with these . . . story lines . . . I agree that Railas has the right to follow them. What has been said can't be unsaid."

Halloran shook his head. "Wow! And you still think this project can just continue, business as usual?"

"I fail to understand why the two of you prioritize my role here as more important than a genuine threat to human life and freedom on this station."

"You're barking up the wrong tree," Halloran said with a shake of his head. "Whatever she told you, this is a non-issue."

"There is the matter of the money in Boaz's account," Rittenhouse admitted. "Close to ten million bits —"

"Ten million?" Halloran coughed. "What the —"

"It's documented." Rittenhouse sighed. "However he got it, Boaz has a fortune we can't account for —"

"That miserable, festering maggot!" Halloran barked. "He's an outsider with no life and a pile of crap somewhere he treats like treasure! He takes a substation to get his fifteen minutes of fame and then ends up needing to be slapped down —"

"I suspect that substation is being used for the most serious of crimes," Railas spoke up. "Now, at this point in my investigation, I'm disposed to think that you were not involved —"

"With an outsider? Of course I'm not involved! What happens outside is not my jurisdiction —"

"Most of the time, perhaps not, but now that I'm bringing this to your attention, you must act."

Halloran considered and then nodded slowly. "Human trafficking," he repeated. "Outside."

"He may be using the substation to host clandestine meetings or 'parties' where humans, particularly women, are forced to participate in acts that even your Sandbox would not allow."

"In the substation?" Halloran scoffed. "Really? A party in a substation?"

"They are modular facilities with operational living space and a well-insulated environment," Railas countered. "The cargo section may also have been modified, or perhaps it was used to handle contraband items, again not available in your downstairs areas."

"And you're getting all this from . . ."

"Eye witness testimony. I plan to corroborate her account with further interviews. Mindy, to start with."

"Mindy?"

"Mindy Pelham," Gibbs mumbled. "Yeah, I looked her up."

Railas turned his attention to him, sensing there was more.

"You're not going to like this," Gibbs said, slightly

downcast. "She's off-station. Has been for at least a month."

Railas remained motionless, his eyes glowing brighter as he scanned his facial features. "And you don't consider that significant?"

"What?" Halloran demanded, turning on Gibbs again.

"The records say what they say," Gibbs shouted. "He'd have subpoenaed them anyway, same with that bank account thing! What do you want from me?"

"Contract completed?" Halloran asked.

Gibbs shook his head. "Early termination."

"After being involved in a tense personnel issue, as I remember," Railas reminded them. "A deal arranged through this office, I might add."

Halloran shook his head and turned back to the window.

"Now, whether or not she was an embarrassment to you personally, she was clearly in a vulnerable position, given the infrequency of shuttles leaving the station, or at least those bound for Earth."

Halloran turned back to him and marched forward. "Just what the hell are you implying?"

"Perhaps nothing," he assured him. "But it's true that you enjoy a situation in which your employees are literally dependent on you for their lives."

His jaw dropped. "How dare you?"

"Easy," he said. "That is my purpose if I read between the lines of my code. You can't threaten me with death or exile. I need no food or oxygen. You have nothing to withhold from me. And, assuming I even *have* a contract you could revoke, I could simply occupy a few meters of space in any closet if it came down to my exile."

Halloran held up his finger, but could not even wag it at him.

"You can't even threaten me with deactivation or destruction," Railas continued. "Not that I relish the idea of not existing, but it doesn't frighten me either. I can't be bribed or threatened. Not even by you."

He looked at Rittenhouse.

"That was one of the project objectives," Rittenhouse admitted.

"Now, seeing as I cannot interview Mindy, I consider it possible, even likely, that she's a victim of Boaz and his associates, wherever they are, which makes my investigation of the substation that much more urgent."

"Investiga . . ." Halloran's jaw dropped again. "You're going outside?"

"Outside," Rittenhouse agreed. "Yeah, that's what he

wants to do."

"Ridiculous!"

"What can you tell me about . . . Wedge?" Railas asked.

All turned to him. "Wedge?" Gibbs asked.

"The gentleman from methane processing who had that relationship with Mindy," Railas clarified.

"Oh, yeah," Gibbs said. "That's Woods. Nate Woods. Wedge is his Sandbox name."

"The man whose hand is now less than functional," Railas realized. "A violent man, as I can personally attest."

"But not a murderer," Gibbs defended.

Railas nodded. "If he were, I doubt he would be that obvious. And right now I'm more concerned with rescuing Mindy."

Halloran chuckled. "Yeah, really? I thought that was a joke."

"Again, I fail to understand your lack of concern," Railas said, raising his voice. "This woman and others could be in danger!"

"Wait! You're angry!" Rittenhouse exclaimed. "You're *really* angry! Over a woman you never actually met." He tried to mask his smile. "This is fantastic!"

"Look, Railas, I appreciate your . . . concern," Gibbs began, walking forward. "But how exactly are you going to rescue Mindy? Where would you even look?"

"I know where the substation must be –"

"And, just like that, you're sure she's there?"

"That is where I will start."

"Do you have any idea what you're even talking about?" Halloran scoffed. He paced randomly for a moment. "Okay, come this way . . ." He pointed to the opposite end of the office. A doorway led to another window, this one overlooking the rear of the dome and the surface of Titan.

In that moment Railas had to concede their point. Looking out at the alien landscape and the murky orange darkness, he couldn't help but realize that he would need more than just strength of purpose.

"I can't protect you out there," Halloran said. "Whatever you think of me, assuming you even do, nobody on this station has come to harm, at least not when they're *inside*. Out there is another matter."

"And that is where the crime must be," Railas agreed.

A shape began to emerge from the darkness, appearing to float in the fog. It was roughly spherical, gliding on the suggestion of a propeller-based suspension system. Behind it was something larger and longer, a blimp-like object holding a great cylinder below it. The tugging vessel guided this object into a parking area holding similar tanks.

"The rules are different out there," Halloran said, taking on his professional, practiced calm. "Low gravity, high pressure. Flying is easy, almost anything becomes buoyant. A ceiling fan could generate enough thrust to get you going. But, beyond that horizon out there, you're lost. No stars for navigation, no functional GPS. That pea soup blocks out everything. That leaves visual beacons, landmarks, and dead reckoning. You fly too high, you get swept up in the high winds, and that's assuming you know how to fly at all. You get lost, good luck. We're all there is on this planet, aside from these substations and the occasional research facility, and wherever the outsiders pitch tent. You don't want to go to them for help, by the way." He tapped his arm. "They use those servos and they'll take every ounce of metal and silicon in your body. They'd eat you up like piranha, have you dismantled and stripped down before you knew what happened. And it's cold out there, colder than you can imagine."

"And Mindy may be lost out there and at their mercy," Railas pointed out. "As I previously mentioned, neither you nor the outsiders can threaten me with death. But, again, if these outsiders would be so cruel to me, how much more might they abuse an untrained and unarmed human female?"

Halloran nodded. "You're a brave . . . robot," he admitted. Then he turned to Gibbs and shrugged. "Put together a team for Sir Lancelot here."

"But . . ." Gibbs stammered.

"You heard him. He's got to save the girl, and so do we. After all, if anyone *does* get hurt out there and it turns out to be former station personnel, it becomes my problem once word gets out."

"The investigation leads there," Rittenhouse admitted. "At this point he must see it through even if it's a dead end. His programming will not allow him to do otherwise."

"Mine would," Gibbs laughed.

"Assemble a team," Halloran repeated. "I'd put you on it, but . . ."

"I'll assemble a team," Gibbs promised. And then the room cleared.

Chapter Thirteen
Outside

Ben Riley leaned close to Railas's chest cavity, pulling the main panel free to expose his circuitry. Amy Noise crouched on the ground next to his right leg, stretching a wide roll of plastic film over his exposed joints, effectively giving him semi-transparent skin.

"You know you still have time to back out," Ben suggested.

"The risk is acceptable."

"You've never been outside," Ben reminded him. "Nobody in here is *ever* prepared for that." He inspected a trunk line of fiber-optic cables before spraying polymer sealant over a collection of circuit boards.

"I appreciate your concern for my safety, but I am designed to survive in a number of environments."

Ben chuckled. "No, my friend, take it from me, I know what I'm talking about. That may be what the brochure says, but it's wrong. You were really only intended to survive in two environments. We found that out the hard way! Yes, you can obviously handle a vacuum, and that covers a lot of places. You can also handle a comfortable Earth-like environment, or some extreme variations of that. But out there on Titan is bizarre-o land!"

"It's cold," Amy agreed.

"So is space," Railas defended. "And hot. There are hundreds of degrees difference between light and shadow."

"Okay, all kidding aside, I'm an engineer," Ben emphasized. "I'm also the only person on this station qualified to work on Robo-Nauts, that's on account of the fact we don't have many. You know why? They're useless out there!"

"Because of radio interference," Railas suggested.

"Like everything else, ten paces away you lose signal," Ben said with an emphatic nod. "So, if you can't see it, you probably can't control it. And if the operator doesn't know where it is and the cameras don't show anything, you're just as lost! But, seriously, we've got a weird environment out there. You're designed to handle the cold, but generally that happens in a vacuum. Here, even in the rigs, you're getting extreme cold *with air pressure*. Air liquefies. That leads to condensation on your boards, frost action, and other nasty things. Normally you cycle with the airlocks. Here I don't know. We have to protect you from moisture and whatever else might seep in. Also, no matter what we do, we're dealing with a higher air pressure outside. We effectively have to reverse your seals."

"The rigs are cold," Amy warned. "Remember, their windows literally contain a layer of ice for insulation. The *maximum* temperature they can be is freezing."

"Cold," Ben repeated. "Optically clear ice, hard as a rock as long as it stays frozen. It gets too warm, the windows collapse."

"So, the interiors of these craft are always below the freezing point of water," Railas understood.

Ben laughed again. "What you've got to understand is there's freezing, right? And then there's *really* freezing! Really freezing is outside, freezing is inside. Then all we have to do is keep warm."

"Those suits the outsiders wear," Railas pondered. "They must be highly insulated."

"Packed with thick polymer gel, yes," Ben agreed. "And each contains a heating unit that circulates channels of hot fluid. We also wear masks to heat the air before we breathe it. You see, if you were going alone, a vacuum would be nice, but it's basically impossible to generate one out there."

Railas turned and looked out the window.

"You've seen those tankers we tow with the rigs, right?"

He nodded.

"Well, without a load, they can do amazing things. And Hell Diver knows how to do most of them!"

"And he's out there now," Railas commented. "Probably destroying evidence, or trying to."

"He's out there," Ben agreed.

"They couldn't hold him," Amy explained. "He wasn't actually accused of anything."

"I can see that," Railas admitted. "But a search warrant would have been nice, and some human guards."

"I can fly one of those," Ben said. "But we need the best for what you propose we do. And *you've* never even flown out there at all."

"Very disorienting," Amy agreed.

"You've got a cabin with a wingspan shorter than your arm, but that's okay," Ben explained. "In the low gravity, staying in the air is easy. And the rig has a propeller system like a swamp boat. You goose the thing and you basically reach escape velocity!"

"That's possible?" Amy asked him.

Ben shrugged. "Hell Diver almost proved it. He saw

the sun at least before working like hell to get back down. He timed the upper winds just right. Dove back down into hell, and somehow found his way home to wherever."

"Titan has no magnetic poles to speak of," Amy reminded him. "Navigation is based on line of site."

"We can orient ourselves along the trade paths," Railas suggested. "I researched how the routes are done. We can follow them until we're close."

Ben nodded. "Wedge will be flying."

"Wedge?" Railas repeated.

"You want the best, right?"

"I'd prefer a pilot whom I *don't* suspect has had a relationship with the victim and possibly the perpetrator we seek to apprehend."

"This is all business," Ben promised. "All he does is get us there and back. I'll be along to keep the rig together and manage getting in and out of the substation. Halloran still wants it back. That means we may have to hitch it up and drag it."

"I'll be coming," Amy said.

"Why?"

"Because I knew Mindy and some of the others. I might be able to identify them."

Railas nodded. "I'd prefer not to expose more people

to danger."

"Too late," Ben chuckled. "What the hell, we could use a joy ride!" And then he set down his tools and dusted off his jacket. "We go out when the next load comes in," he promised as he left the room.

Railas then felt Amy's hand on his fingers. "You're brave," she said. And her look conveyed the same sense of connection McClusky's had. "I didn't know Mindy was gone," she admitted. "I don't think anybody knew. She'd made mistakes, but . . ."

"We'll bring her back," Railas promised. "At least five others could be there as well. And then I'm certain we can make a case for the company to return them to Earth. I'll do it even if I have to contact Mr. Horgan himself."

"Railas, I'm . . . sorry," she said.

"Why? You couldn't have known that Mindy was in danger."

"No, I'm sorry because I know all these tests we put you through . . . Well, I just don't want you to think we don't respect you."

"I don't know why you would," Railas admitted. "As a non-human I doubt I have much in the way of status."

"But you do. You're proving it now. Even *they* didn't know. You really care about Mindy. Literally nobody

137

else does. I just want you to know that it matters to me."

"Then you care as well."

She nodded. Then she gently touched the polymer skin she had applied to his arm, stretching it over a joint that was partially exposed.

Chapter Fourteen
Take Off

The exit hangar on the other side of Halloran's office was a cold, cavernous room separated from the rest of the colony by several feet of insulated wall. Each step down the corridor leading to the hangar was accompanied by a sharp drop in temperature. Beyond the reinforced door and vestibule was a cold that resembled winter on Earth, or a large walk-in freezer. Now their steps crunched as the imperfect gravity pressed their feet against frost and dry ice.

Railas, aside from his new skin, was not dressed differently than usual, but the others clearly were. The suits they wore were a way of life for the outsiders and apparently the dock workers as well. They were thick, jointed armor, and their plates were painted different colors depending on department allegiances and other criteria Railas didn't know. Comically, now the humans looked every bit as mechanical as Railas did.

The Rig was a specialized vehicle that would make no sense anywhere other than Titan. It resembled a helicopter in that its main cabin included a transparent bubble in front connected to a less glamorous rear cargo section. The vehicle could also be mistaken for a truck from distance, a rear bed providing a means of carrying freight. It also included a crane and a winch mechanism for towing. Like a helicopter, it rested on skis rather than wheels and there were rudder-like projections which may have functioned as wings.

The door to the bubble cabin was open, its hinges amazingly large. On Earth the door might have weighed close to a ton, its six inch width laden with glass and ice. Standing in front of the door was an unwelcome sight.

"Mr. Woods," Railas called out. "I hope your hand is healing nicely."

Woods sneered at him, raising his right arm in an obscene gesture. "Just who do you think you are?" he demanded. "You're here for, what, a week? And now you're turning the whole place upside down!"

Railas practiced his shrug, his shoulders unencumbered by clothing or other gear. "I'm sorry my active investigation inconveniences you, Mr. Woods. I understand you go by the name 'Wedge' as well. Just how do you humans keep track of all these names?"

"Good question," Ben admitted, his words letting out

a cloud of steam.

"But you're *upstairs* now," Railas commented to Woods. "I see a change of clothes makes a big difference around here. I imagine you wear an entirely different outfit in methane processing."

"We all have to wear a few hats around here," he said with a smug grin.

"And you also fly these vehicles," Railas said, indicating the rig. "I still would prefer another pilot if possible."

"I thought you might feel that way," Woods said. "And, unless I was taking you to a scrap yard somewhere, I wouldn't want to ride with you either. But the fact is Halloran's pissed off and I owe him. He also doesn't want *more* trouble. And the last thing he needs now is a lost rig and dead newbies! Yes, even you." He indicated Railas.

"I'm touched," Railas lied. "But you're actually involved in this investigation. We're looking for Mindy, and I don't know for sure that you weren't involved with her disappearance."

"Mindy?" he asked, his face registering surprise. "What has she got to do with . . . What are you even talking about?"

"She's missing."

"How can she be missing?" he laughed. "She left the planet weeks ago!"

Railas shook his head. "Not verified."

"What the hell are you accusing me of?"

"I can't directly accuse you of anything yet," Railas admitted. "But you may be involved in criminal conspiracy, kidnapping, and general space piracy."

"That's a good one!" he laughed. "Piracy?"

"It fits," Railas confirmed. "In fact, most of the outsiders are running illegal rackets of one kind or another."

"What, card games? Is that what this is about? They're a bunch of idiots! Just kids and losers, mostly, out wondering the wasteland because nobody'd hire them to do anything else! But they *do* know how to survive out there, which is more than I can say for you three."

"And Halloran expects *you* to keep us safe?" Amy asked.

Woods sighed. "I'm to run you out to the mystery spot where you expect to see that substation, verify that nothing's there, and bring you back. I do that and I don't owe him a favor anymore."

"And what qualifies you to do that?" Railas asked, still unsatisfied.

"I was an outsider before there *were* outsiders, so I know the game. There was a time when we had to find our own Methane sources and couldn't farm it out to losers like Hell Diver."

"Hell Diver may be a pirate, but I wouldn't say he's a loser. Not anymore," Railas said. "He currently has enough money to buy out your contract several times over."

"Bull!"

"And, however he earned that money, it has nothing to do with running methane in an already saturated market. On the other hand, the type of 'parties' he seems to be putting on out there could be extremely lucrative with the right kind of customers. That and drug trafficking and we get the whole picture."

"He thinks Mindy is in the substation," Amy explained. "And he's got Halloran convinced there might be something to this."

"Is Mindy in the substation?" Railas asked Woods.

He sighed. "How would I know? We broke up a long time ago."

"And we still don't know the whole story about that, do we?"

Woods took a step closer to Railas, and it almost

appeared that he might strike him again. Instead, he only pointed at him. "I don't like you," he grumbled. "But I never hurt Mindy. I don't know what they told you, but I never did. I thought she left. If she didn't . . ."

Railas nodded. "Then you deny being involved with this?"

"Yeah, I deny it, what do you want from me?"

"You are a contradiction," Railas said after a pause. "I see no evidence that you are lying concerning Mindy's whereabouts. At the same time I can find little indication that you care what has become of her."

"We broke up," he repeated.

"It was a while ago," Amy said. "And some men aren't the . . . emotional type."

"At least not those emotions." Railas nodded.

Woods then motioned to the rig. "Get in and attach your breathers," he ordered. Then he looked at Railas. "Not you, of course. Just . . . don't breathe."

When the door was closed the capsule became remarkably quiet, the layers of glass and ice insulating them from sound as well as cold. Woods took his seat at the controls in the front of the bubble. Railas and Amy took the two seats behind his, while Ben occupied the back, operating a console that gave him what navigation details were available.

"The windy season hasn't hit yet," he announced. "But expect precipitation. I called for launch, so we'll be out in a minute."

And then the rig began to move forward, not by engine power, but something else. The floor on which they sat was part of a conveyor system and it was moving them towards the exit. Railas could already detect further temperature drops. The breathers Ben spoke of would be necessary to keep the cabin air in a completely gaseous state.

At the end of the main belt another carried them beyond the door, which closed behind them. And then the outer door opened to reveal chaos. The murky atmosphere outside swirled ahead of them, visibly shaking a nearby weather vain. And, as the final conveyor took them beyond the foundation, gravity released them and the engines purred. They were aloft almost instantly, lurching forward as the main propeller engaged. More cold outside and a kind of rain that made no sense. Droplets bounced off the bubble like water on a hot skillet, some beading up and dancing, others fizzling out as the meager heat from inside caused them to evaporate. The hangar disappeared behind them almost immediately, reduced only to the few spotlights outlining the door and the lights in the windows. Seconds more and these grew faint as well. Eventually even the great dome threatened to wink out as the fog thickened. Simultaneously, a dim light appeared ahead of them, the first of many markers.

"Leaving Shangri-La on a vector of 270," Ben announced. "We'll follow the beaten path until we reach marker 37."

Amy shivered in spite of herself. "Wow, I never thought I'd see this."

"See what?" Woods mocked. "Rocks?"

"So you're saying you get no help from satellite navigation?" Railas asked. "Surely we can go to a particular set of coordinates."

"What planet are *you* living on?" Woods grumbled. "Titan barely has a magnetic field, and the one it has competes with Saturn's. You can *try* to navigate that way, but you have to be damn good at it! We have a saying here. 'Keep the light in sight.' And, if we *do* have to go off the marked path, we drop lights of our own."

Railas craned his neck, looking back the way they had come. One light from the station was barely visible. It was a pulsing light that left a trail in the fog. An old-fashioned light house. And then the craft angled upward.

The rocky surface nearly vanished beneath the bubble even at low altitude, and all they could see was an endless parade of smooth stones and pebbles. The sun was visible as a smudge in the orange fog. Perhaps that was what Hell Diver had risked his life to see, a glimpse of the sun as he knew it from Earth. Railas could imagine the need to do so.

Chapter Fifteen
The Hiding Place

The rig's headlights barely mattered in the muddy orange haze as the rig glided towards the blank horizon. Now that they were off the trail of lights, only the passing of the ground below them indicated they were moving at all, and the occasional gust of wind would take them high enough to lose even that. The dancing rain continued, blown by silent winds. Behind them, a trail of lighting beacons provided their only means of retracing their steps. Even the lighthouse at the top of Shangri-La was only a faint glow, if visible at all.

"Nothing yet," Ben announced from the back. "No electrical signature, nothing."

"It must be here," Railas insisted. "Unless he moved it, of course."

"Not likely," Woods grunted. "We generally know where the outsiders are, based on known traffic. Even *they* have to follow the markers sometimes. This is not a popular spot. Chances are it was never here to begin with."

The rig wobbled as its fins and propellers adjusted to the direction of the wind, keeping a relative position with the ground below. But then the rocks ahead disappeared.

"What's that?" Amy asked, wide-eyed in amazement.

Ahead was a sight they would likely see nowhere else. Below the murky sky was a shimmering blue pool stretching out ahead of them, dark, but reflecting the cloud patterns above. The suggestion of waves punctuated the surface, but the shore was calm and still.

"A methane lake, no kidding!" Ben said. "You don't see that every day. Actually, it's the only one around here. Most of them are up north."

"So that's actual methane?" Amy asked.

"Crude methane," Woods amended. "Ethane as well, and a few other compounds. Full of salts most of the time, especially the ones up north."

"This lake was on my map," Railas said. "The substation should be around here somewhere."

Woods pulled back on the controls, causing the rig to hover against the varying winds. He then gently brought the craft down, its skis kissing the ground in the light gravity.

"The markers we dropped are rated for only a few hours," Woods warned. "We're going to need to turn tail and head back soon. Congratulations, Railas, you've reached the magic spot on your map. If the thing was here, we'd see it."

But Railas wasn't convinced. He stood, looking around the top of the bubble, his vision cycling through various modes. He looked up at the tall rocks on shore, not sure what he expected to see. The wind and waves would have erased any previous tracks that might have been in the sand, or any traces that anyone besides them had been there at all. It was possible they were the first to see this section of Titan. But then Railas directed his attention forward again.

"I see something," he said. "Out there."

Ben laughed. "When you say 'out there' do you meant *out there*, out there?"

"I'm getting electro magnetics and a slight heat signature," he announced.

"In the lake?" Ben asked. "How is that possible?"

"It appears they submerged the substation in the methane lake," Railas said.

Wood coughed. "Are you nuts?"

"Actually, yeah, I suppose they could do that," Ben defended. "The systems were designed to work at that temperature, and they're sealed enough to hold back the pressure, at least in shallow areas. Heck, it might even act as an insulator. But it'd be pretty hard to do, that's for sure! And they'd never get it out of there!"

"Got that right," Woods agreed. "It would be suicide to even try. That station would be toast, plain and simple. If that's what he did, all Halloran can do is charge him for it. He seems to have the money . . ."

"They can't pull it out?" Amy spoke up. "I mean, if it's down there?"

"No, the suction would make that impossible, assuming you could even find it," Ben said, turning to her. "Like any lake, these bodies of liquid have mud associated with them. Not what you might think of as mud, but it has the same characteristics. No, they'd have no way of getting leverage."

"You're missing the point," Railas spoke up. "Even at close range, none of you spotted this with your equipment, and even now it's virtually undetectable. If you wanted to hide evidence, I can think of no better way to do it."

Woods turned to him. "You're still on that kick, are you? This is a prank, not a crime! Let's say he knew he'd eventually have to give the substation back. Let's say he even dumped it there recently to *avoid* giving it back. It's just his way of giving Halloran the finger. The man isn't that complicated."

"I didn't say he was," Railas agreed. "There's nothing complicated about disposing of evidence. You humans have been hiding bodies at the bottoms of lakes and oceans for centuries. Here it's even more effective. There's virtually no chance that anyone would happen upon anything down there. There are no fishing boats on this lake, or casual swimmers. The fact that we're here is an amazing event in itself."

"Well, there *is* something out there," Ben agreed. "He's right, I'm detecting a metallic reading nearby. It would take something about that big to register from here."

"The reading should grow stronger the closer we get," Railas said. "Direct your instruments downward, use that ghost reading as a guide. Let's go," he said to Woods.

"What?" Woods shouted. "Are you kidding me?" He motioned ahead of them. "You want to go out there?"

"Those were your orders, if I'm not mistaken. That's what Halloran is paying you to do, in whatever currency you trade in."

Woods shook his head. "Do you know how many regulations that would violate? I can't fly above a lake or any body of liquid, there are whole pages of regs against that!"

"He's right," Ben agreed. "Once we're over the lake, making a forced landing becomes a lot more complicated. We wouldn't sink, but we could fowl the engines."

"And our markers would be useless!" Woods laughed.

"Oh, no, those would work," Ben said. "They'd float for a while, but they might drift some –"

"We won't have to go out very far," Railas assured them. "If I'm right, the substation is only partially submerged, or close to the surface. This lake isn't very deep."

"We're talking about our lives!" Woods insisted. "You don't know how dangerous it can be out here, do you? We need to start heading back now."

"We will," Railas promised. "But we must have something to report."

"I agree," Ben spoke up. "Like he said, I don't think this'll be far ahead. A few minutes, not much more than that. I mean, what would be the sense in coming all the way out here and not going those last few meters? We at least need to know if it's worth another trip."

"Could they be in there?" Amy asked. "The missing people?"

Railas nodded.

"Alive?"

"The stations are self-contained," Ben said. "Even submerged, they'd still be insulated. Wouldn't be easy, but yeah, it'd be possible for a while."

"Fly," Railas demanded.

Woods looked from one face to another, even Railas's, and then turned back to the controls. "I'm turning back the moment this becomes a danger," he insisted. "I'm not going to die for a treasure hunt!"

Beyond the shore, Railas understood his concern. The lake's surface lost all definition below them, making it hard to tell what direction they were flying in. They could see the reflection of the craft in the lake, but little else. The only surface ripples were generated by their own engines. Additional markers would be far less effective, and could even lead them astray. Only the ones on shore were truly reliable. Hell Diver was either brave or stupid to take such chances, but he'd chosen a way of life that gave him a unique perspective. Perhaps such challenges were gratifying in themselves.

"Wow, that's a picture!" Amy said, her face beaming.

And so it was. The lake reflected not just their ship, but also the sky. And, even with the haze, Saturn was hard to miss through the clouds, its reflected light providing a beacon in the twilight. But then a klaxon sounded.

"Woah," Ben spoke up. "Now *that's* a reading!"

Woods pulled back on the controls, bringing them to hover. The pool below was dark and murky, but there was a suggestion of something underneath, something large.

"Why that son of a . . ." Woods shook his head. "Looks like you nailed it, Railas. Halloran got his money's worth on you, I'll say that. He's not getting *that* substation back, but at least he'll know where it is!"

"Lower," Railas said. "Take us lower."

"Are you crazy?" he laughed. "Didn't you hear what Ben said? We get those engines wet or get swept up in air currents, we stall!"

"Down!" Railas shouted. "We need a closer look."

"Take us down another few feet," Ben agreed. "I think I see what he's talking about."

Woods sighed, grasping the engine controls. They began descending, meeting their reflection below. And then even Woods knew what Railas meant. The waves, both natural and those created by their thrust, were mostly smooth, but were breaking in one spot. Something was reaching up from below. And it had a regular shape.

"Is that what I think it is?" Ben spoke up first.

"What do you think it is?" Amy asked.

"It's a regress hatch," Railas said. "The substation has

at least one point of exit on its upper most section. This one appears to have been extended in such a way as to rise just above the methane surface. This was deliberate." He rested his hand on Woods' shoulder. "Halloran's substation was not being disposed of. It appears to be in use."

"But . . . " Ben stammered. "How would anyone get in and out? We can't swim in this stuff, that would be suicide!"

"The same way *we'll* get in," Railas said. "We dock the rig, that's what the hatch is for. It's intended to be an entry port. Our lower hatch should be able to form a seal. You'll find it by your feet," he said to Ben."

"You want me to touch down?" Woods laughed, not even bothering to shout. "Seriously, this isn't some kind of dream I'm having?"

"You claim to be a good pilot," Railas said. "I'll speak to Halloran about your valor. Perhaps he will now owe *you* a favor."

"He'll owe me a truck load!"

"Take your time," Ben said. "The wind is calm at least, you should be able to do it. I'll guide you."

"Take us down," Railas said. Amy nodded as well.

"Damn!" Woods whispered. But then he grasped the

controls and the tiny spot below them began to enlarge.

Chapter Sixteen
Impossible Hideaway

The rig spiraled against the wind, churning up liquid as its propellers fought to keep position, some splashing on the lower part of the bubble window in a spectacle of steam.

"Damn!" Woods barked. "I told you! That stuff gets on the engines and we're screwed!"

"Not to worry," Ben said from behind him. "You'd have to pretty much submerge the engines to lose them. A splash alone wouldn't do it. Just keep us level."

Railas glanced at the two forward engines, noting that the propellers were deflecting what droplets were hitting them, and the engines themselves appeared well sealed. The exposed hatch was clearly defined below them now, but it would have been impossible to see from even a few feet higher than they had originally been. For a hiding place, this was a masterpiece. But it had one obvious weakness: It worked both ways. Railas couldn't imagine how anyone inside could see them approaching. In the fog, the rig would be just as hard to make out from the ground as the tiny hatch had been from above. Even with cameras and other surveillance equipment, a few feet would have made them invisible until they had pretty much docked. Hopefully that would prove to be an advantage.

The hatch was a circular opening, like a manhole in the street, but it had a standard size and shape and included fittings for the rig's docking clamps. All the way down Woods cursed under his breath, his hands cramping as he fought with the controls. When they did finally touch down they could feel the mass of the ship for the first time. Though floating on the wind like a child's balloon, the rig weighed several tons, and its mass was very real. When the two objects connected, the ship settled hard, like two bricks striking each other or a weight lifter setting down a particularly heavy barbell. But the seal was established. Suddenly the ship felt solid and motionless, and the view outside became stable. They were then given a vista not unlike that of a beach house overlooking a shimmering lake. The colors were different than they would be on Earth, but they were just as striking.

Ben struggled with the floor plates to expose the lower hatch, which may never have been used before. His fingers were encumbered by gloves and Railas had to help him grip the valve and turn it, releasing the door to what waited below. It popped open as pressurized liquid methane evaporated in the warmer air. The rotten egg smell was mild but obvious even through their breathers.

The hatch below theirs opened downward into a cylindrical chamber. A crude ladder was available, but was scarcely necessary in the micro gravity.

"I'll go first," Railas offered. "In case we meet resistance I would be harder to destroy."

"Doesn't matter," Ben countered. "In these suits we're all pretty safe, and I can't imagine they'd be expecting us."

"There could be traps," Railas suggested, "or other measures to repel intruders. In there *we* are the outsiders. Whether they expected us or not, they may well have prepared some kind of response for situations like this. And they could know we're here by now."

"Can't argue with that," Ben agreed.

"Do we have weapons?" Railas asked.

Woods laughed. "You kidding? You mean guns? Welcome to Titan! Try flying anything heavy like that out here, let alone bullets! Even station security is lucky to have stun pistols! And, whatever guns they *do* have, they wouldn't waste them on a suicide mission like this. And they didn't even know it *was* a suicide mission!" He laughed again. "Don't worry; even the outsiders don't have much by way of armaments. Pretty much we have numbers, harsh language, and the fact that they don't *know* what we have and don't have."

"Can you radio back to the station?" Amy asked.

Woods shook his head. "Not from here, not with our antenna system. We'd have to bounce off the satellite to have a chance, and that's almost never possible."

"But they know where we are, right?"

He shrugged. "No, they know about where we were heading, but even *we* don't know where we are exactly. If we don't turn up they'll send another team, but . . . Well, let's just not hang around too long."

Ben reached the bottom of the tube and paused at another hatch. Woods went in next, followed by Amy and Railas, who secured the hatch above them. Should the rig become dislodged from the port, that door would be all that would hold back a potential flood of liquid methane.

The inner hatch led farther down, through several feet of insulated wall. Somewhere down there was light. Ben looked up at them and nodded. They did use the ladder this time, guiding themselves down through layers of solid hull, growing warmer as they descended. When their feet touched the floor beneath the low ceiling they could no longer see their breath in the air.

Amy took off her breather first and nodded. Not only was the temperature above freezing, it was surprisingly warm and free of the methane smell they had experienced above. The room was empty aside from a bench where one might store gear. Another hatchway led to the interior of the station. Beyond this door would be answers.

The clamps on the door were secured hard, and may not have been opened recently, but they could feel the vibration of the life support system. This station was home to somebody, or at least it could be. And Ben was able to turn the clamp with his bare hands.

Inside was yet another surprise. Stepping through a curtain, they emerged into a room that resembled the Sandbox on a slow day. For a home away from home, the décor was far better than what might be expected in a holding cell. Railas pondered. Yes, a person with eccentric tastes in entertainment, particularly those that venture into the dark side of humanity might seek seclusion, but what he saw before him would require more than mere cunning and thievery. It was also completely incongruous with human trafficking. This was luxury far beyond what would even be possible on Shangri-La. Something was very wrong with what he saw. A large piece of the puzzle was missing, and the more he saw, the less sense it made.

The room looked like a common living area, though any windows were naturally absent. Other rooms farther in could be accessed through a central corridor. The furniture included plush couches and chairs that might actually be too soft in micro-gravity. And even one of these items would cost a fortune to ship if it could be done at all. The lighting fixtures were also large, some of them floor lamps, covered with decorative paper shades, completely impractical in space.

"This is impossible," Ben exclaimed. He rested his hand on a chair. "This is real wood! I mean *real* wood, not pressed ceramic or something like that. Even Halloran couldn't have something like this. We thought he was rich because he had a wooden clock and a picture frame! And *all* these chairs are wood!"

"And those tapestries are real, too," Amy said, feeling the weave of what may have been an antique wall hanging of an ocean scene. "That's woven cloth." She sniffed it. "Old woven cloth. And the carpet . . ." She brushed her feet on the floor, testing the resistance of the fibers.

"It would appear that Hell Diver has been doing quite well for himself," Railas said. "Impossibly so."

The lighting was warm, in contrast to what they would expect to see on any space station, though the gravity was still low. As they proceeded down the hallway they could see the same décor in the other rooms. Not like jail cells, as Railas expected, but more like hotel rooms, the master suite being at the end. And then came the real shock. A man waited to greet them.

All froze. Most humans who ventured into space were not particularly large. Whether this had to do with the cost of space travel or the physical challenges that came with it Railas wasn't sure. But the man who stood before him was stout and far from athletic. He also showed no signs of the bone ailments associated with micro-gravity. Another impossibility. This man would be completely out of place on Shangri-La or any place nearby. He wore a well-fitting gray suit which, if available at all this far from Earth, would cost more than could be imagined by most.

He smiled over his double chin. "Well, this is unexpected." He held a drink in his hand, and he took a sip from it. His cup was not globular, nor was it made out of plastic. It was genuine glass and looked like something one would only find on Earth. It also included ice cubes, which, though not unknown on Titan, were different in shape. The man nodded to each of them with an expression of amusement. "It appears my associate has a few things to learn about redundant security."

"Is your associate Hell Diver?" Railas asked.

The man looked surprised at Railas's words, as if not expecting him to speak first. "A little man with a big name," he agreed. "Miserable runt, but he's been known to do as he's told."

"Harmy Boaz," Railas added.

"That his real name?" He shrugged. "Doesn't matter. Sometimes the most useless people can be useful if you find out what it is they want."

"And what did Hell Diver want?" Railas asked.

He shook his head. "Confidential, of course."

Ben stepped forward, looking closer at their host. "You . . ."

"I believe we have the distinction of addressing Mr. Cornelius Horgan," Railas said. "Only his particular kind of wealth could buy all this."

"You're well read," the man admitted.

"But that's impossible!" Ben shouted. "All the way from Earth? And he comes out here just to hide in . . ."

"A methane lake," Railas finished for him. "Yes, 'impossible' would be the right word. Or improbable at

165

least."

"Impossible is a meaningless term," Horgan said, taking another sip of his drink. "Lazy people use that word. Some of us choose to ignore it. That's how we get things done." He grinned. "Though, admittedly, the impossible takes just a bit more work." He waved his glass, as if proposing a toast to the room. "Possible," he insisted. "My frontier town, as some call it, is no more or less remarkable than any other vision worth working for. And, like the original frontier, it can take on other dimensions besides industry alone."

Railas nodded. "Downstairs," he suggested.

Horgan chuckled. "You do get around, don't you? You know, even Halloran doesn't know what goes on down there, though he thinks he does. But he does try, doesn't he? But, no, this is more like outside, up the block, over into the next county, and downstairs again!"

"A brothel, I take it?" Railas suggested.

"Could be." He shrugged. "Or anything else you want, too, and more. It's a place to entertain our more important clients, and a place where they can be reasonably sure of not being . . . observed, so to speak. Halloran's good at that, by the way. That whole 'inside outside' stuff is perfect for something like this. That's why

I hired a prison man. They're trained to look the other way."

"I was wrong about him," Railas admitted. "I thought Halloran might have been behind this. No way it could have been just Boaz. To be honest I never considered you."

"I don't know whether to be complimented or insulted." He chuckled. "But it seems Rittenhouse's little project turned out to be more interesting than I first thought."

"Were you behind that as well?" Railas asked.

"Yes and no." Horgan shrugged. "I deal in people, not so much ideas. Rittenhouse had an idea, I was curious to see where it would go, so . . ."

"But you didn't expect it to go this far, did you?" Amy asked.

Horgan smiled at her. "No, my dear, I did not. That said, it's always nice to know what's on the horizon. Another card in *my* hand is one that can't be played against me. But look at you, mister legal beagle!" He indicated Railas. "You've solved the case you were never given, put your metal nose where nobody wanted it, and you unraveled the *real* mystery! And, like the brave instrument of justice you are, I assume you'd arrest even me." He set his glass down on a table and extended his hands as if offering them to be cuffed.

"I don't have arrest powers," Railas said. "But, yes, I would take legal action against you, assuming you're guilty of crimes."

"Justice!" he remarked, clapping his hands. "Even now you don't jump to conclusions. Rittenhouse was right! You'd scare the hell out of any outsider who stepped out of line, and even Halloran couldn't out deal you!"

"Where's Mindy?" Railas demanded.

Horgan nodded. "Yeah, that was something he mentioned as well. Some fascination with a low level . . . secretary I think . . . Someone who never meant anything to anybody –"

"She's a citizen and a human being!" Railas shouted, realizing that he could. "And she has the same rights as you do!" And then he did something he thought he never would. His hand make a fist and he shook it at Horgan. Was this truly anger?

He took a step closer to Horgan. "Was she here? Is she here? What happens to people here? Where do they go?"

Horgan watched, but didn't take a step back. He

nodded. "Yeah, they said something about simulated emotions. Good stuff."

"Answer me!"

He shrugged. "Where do they go? Believe it or not, sloppy book keeping, mostly."

"I *don't* believe it," Railas said. "Where are the women who were seen here? They were never seen again on the station, so where did they go? Are there other similar enclaves?"

Just then Woods put his hand on Railas's shoulder. "Shut up!" he whispered into what he assumed was a microphone on the side of his head. "You want to get us killed?"

Railas turned to him.

"We don't *want* to know, if you know what I mean."

"Secrets," Horgan said, clapping his hands. "Very well, I can't resist! Do you actually know where we are?"

"Yes."

"And how do you suppose I got here?"

Railas shrugged. "I don't know the details of your travels –"

"Have you ever heard of Quantum Entanglement technology?"

"You've got a QEC here?" Ben perked up. "Instant

communication with Earth? I've always wanted to see one of those! From the station, assuming we can even get a signal through, it takes almost an hour each way. That's a long time to wait checking your email!"

Horgan smiled. "My company *owns* QEC, or at least enough of it that we might as well. And we hold all the important patents, too, most notably, QET."

"You're kidding!" Ben laughed. "That's impossible!"

"There's that word again!" Horgan grinned. "Again, it just takes a little more doing. But it's actually simpler than you might think, though very expensive to set up. All we need is an archway with only a right side, not a left side."

"But that's impos . . ." Ben looked from one face to another. "Isn't it?"

"Quantum entanglement involves particles that appear to be connected even when they are great distances apart," Railas explained. "This phenomenon has been used to transmit simple information, where modifying a particle on one side can cause a predictable reaction on the other side."

"Da dat, da, da dat!" Horgan sang, mimicking the sound of Morse code. "Such a small breakthrough, but yeah, that one brought in a bundle of cash!"

"But you're talking about something else," Ben ventured. "Something bigger . . . "

"At last you see." Horgan's grin vanished. "QEC requires only one particle in theory. QET, on the other hand, requires matter. Lots of it! A door, basically, with only one side. And, of course, we have the other half of that archway back on Earth."

"Impossible," Ben whispered again, but with far less confidence.

"So, you can teleport to Earth and back?" Railas asked.

"In a matter of speaking," he said. "You could also say that half of this suite is already there."

"That would explain how you can furnish this apartment so lavishly," Ben agreed.

"It works out to be far cheaper than space travel. That's one of the reasons we keep it under our hat."

"Mindy is back on Earth, then," Railas concluded. "Along with all the others."

"Is that really what you want to know?"

"I want to see her!" Railas demanded.

"Oh, you do go on, don't you?" he grumbled, as if growing tired of an annoying student pressing the same point.

171

"So do I," Amy spoke up, standing closer to Railas. "I want to see *all* of them! I have a list. We want to see everyone who's missing."

Horgan looked over at her, and then at Railas. "Why?"

"That's why we came here," Railas said. "We believe there has been a crime committed and that these women have been abused. Until we know otherwise this is still a criminal investigation."

Horgan laughed within his throat. "Criminal . . . Uhm, . . . not to burst your bubble, but you can't have crimes without laws, now can you? Just what jurisdiction would you say we're in right now?"

Railas answered without pause. "Law practiced out here is based on internationally agreed upon statutes governing space piracy –"

"Which not every nation agrees with," Horgan scoffed. "And it could be successfully argued that *this* place is outside the operating radius of Shanri-La, and therefore does not fall under the same jurisdiction. Think frontier!" He laughed. "You're in the wilderness where anything goes! What, are you the new sheriff?" He leaned closer to him. "Problem is, you have to *earn* that shiny badge."

"You speak of jurisdiction," Railas commented. "Legal versus illegal. In which jurisdiction is slavery legal? That and rape?"

"I could probably name a few–"

"My point exactly," he interrupted. "But that doesn't make them right! And, yes, right and wrong are not just concepts, but the foundation for every law that exists. They're more basic than laws. They're the deciding factor concerning whether or not *any* law is legitimate or the whim of some feudal dictator. And this moral compass, this basic Geiger counter of right and wrong, must become *all* important on this frontier you speak of. Justice out here depends on it. But let me phrase our question another way: We want to see Mindy because she is our friend. We'd like to know how she's doing because she matters to us, whether you care for her or not. Is that possible?"

Horgan sighed and looked away, as if losing interest in the conversation. "No, sheriff, it is not."

"Why not?"

"Because I say it's not," he said, crossing his arms in front of him. "This is *my* world, Sheriff Railas, and my rules." He gestured with his chin at the room. "And this is what you would call a company town."

Railas nodded. "I thought as much."

173

Woods had been trying to get Railas's attention for several moments, and at this he kicked him hard on the leg. "Shut up!" he whispered.

"Have you forgotten how you hurt your hand?" Railas asked, not looking to him.

"No, *you* shut up," Horgan regarded Woods. "Nobody cares what you have to say."

"We work for Halloran," Woods said. "If we can just go back to Shangri-La –"

"No, Mr. Woods, I don't give a damn who you work for. Why the hell would I?" he said, growing more annoyed.

"No, I suppose you wouldn't," Railas agreed. He turned to Amy. "In case you were wondering about this man, I think I can introduce him as the closest equivalent to the devil that you are likely to meet. Someone who believes that right and wrong are arbitrary must, by his nature, be evil."

Amy looked to Woods and Ben with concern, perhaps now understanding Wood's warning. "We still want to know about Mindy," she said, straightening up.

And then his eyes seemed to brighten and he smiled. "Well, perhaps I can arrange something here in our master suite," he suggested. "I didn't say I couldn't make her appear, or others like her."

Amy blushed, and Railas noticed her body temperature rise. "Pig," she whispered.

His face darkened. "You had to make this personal, didn't you? It isn't, you know. You see, on the frontier, some commodities are scarce." He subtly looked Amy up and down. "And some people *become* commodities. And, sheriff or no, this place belongs to me."

And then, as if to punctuate his words, the room shook. Only Ben recognized the cause.

"That's a pressure break!" he shouted.

Horgan smiled. "At least one of you has a brain, I see." He glanced up at the ceiling. "I just opened the valves in the escape tunnel you so valiantly entered. There are now several hundred gallons of liquid methane between you and the surface. I'm afraid your colleague was right, there are some secrets we *don't* want getting out."

"You bastard!" Woods shouted. He then ran at Horgan, who moved with surprising dexterity, unencumbered by armor plating. Sparks sizzled from his hand as a small taser barked. And then Horgan stepped to the side, disappearing behind a narrow doorway he had never been more than one stride away from. A fortified door clamped shut behind him.

"Is that the . . . ?"

"Could be," Railas said. "If he's right about Quantum Entanglement Transport, such a thing would be heavy, but not unlike any other metal."

"We've got to get out of here!" Amy said, breathing hard.

"Indeed we do," Railas agreed. "And I think there may be a way. But we'll have to move quickly!"

Chapter Seventeen
Specifications

Ben examined the mysterious door, feeling the edge of the frame experimentally and pushing on the metal. Woods paced like an angry tiger in a cage. Amy grasped one of the chairs and seemed to be gauging whether or not it could be turned into a weapon.

"I don't think you'll be able to open that door," Railas said to Ben. "If what he said is true, I'm sure that way would be completely under his control. I suspect it can only be opened from his side."

"QET is not a valid science," Ben said, as if in denial. "And even if it wasn't, how can it be that simple?"

"Some of the most important things ever discovered are just that simple," Railas mused. "But right now we have other concerns."

"He's coming back, isn't he?" Amy whispered, her face growing pale. "With others . . ."

"Yes," Railas agreed, grasping her shoulders. "And, yes, we can't afford to be here when that happens. But either way he'll have to completely dismantle me before

177

I'll let him do to you what he did to the others."

Woods snorted. "Good luck! That's not how the game is played."

"And I'm sure you're quite familiar with this game," Railas taunted, not looking in his direction.

"It's the control game, you naïve idiot!" he shot back. "That man is one of *those* bastards and we're in the box! We climb in, he shuts the door and then watches us stagger around like a bunch of morons!" He grabbed the tapestry Amy had been looking at and ripped it from the wall. "Don't you see? It doesn't matter what he did or didn't do to Mindy, all that matters is what we *think* he did! He wants us afraid!" He savagely whipped the nearest chair with the remains of the tapestry, churning dust and threads in all directions. "He's probably got all kinds of tricks to show us who's boss." He kicked over one of the chairs and pushed the table against the wall. "He could turn out the lights, turn off the heat, play all kinds of Halloween sounds, stuff like that! All the while, he's sitting in an easy chair somewhere sipping campaign and puffing a big fat cigar that costs more than my contract!"

"That is *exactly* why this is unacceptable!" Railas said, finally turning to him. "You humans amaze me! You come all the way out here, supposedly to create some comfortable, efficient mini-society, and the first thing you do is bring all your vices with you, while at the same time pretending they don't exist!" He began to pace, his eyes searching every corner of the room for new dangers. "Half of you create underworlds where you revel in taboo and contraband while the other half compete with each other to come up with greater and greater ways of subjugating and oppressing you." He stopped and faced them. "Well, somebody somewhere programed me to put a stop to that. I don't know who that was, but it certainly wasn't any of you."

Woods laughed again. "What are you, a super hero? Truth, justice, and the American way?"

"Why not?" he asked. "What's wrong with truth and justice? And this American culture you reference was never perfect, but it *is* based on freedom and self-determination. It's *wrong* to mistreat people in this fashion, and we can't allow it to continue."

"I hate to break it to you," Ben mumbled, "but I don't think we can do much about this. I'm not even sure the rig is still up there, and these suits can't protect us from *that* kind of cold, let alone wade through liquid methane." He picked up Horgan's discarded drink and sniffed it. "He flooded the damned escape tube! That means we're stuck here. Even opening that hatch *a crack* could get us all killed!"

"We're dead anyway," Woods grunted. "Weren't you listening? We know too much! I tried to warn you! Any minute now that door's gonna open up and a gang of thugs is gonna come in with guns. And that's if we're lucky!"

"He won't kill *me*," Amy said, looking down. "God knows what happened to Mindy."

Railas studied their faces one by one, again feeling genuine anger. "No," he insisted. "This is *not* acceptable." He turned to Ben, who was studying the door again. He grasped his arm, turning him to face him. "Benjamin, you're an engineer, correct?"

He shrugged.

"We have a problem to solve, and I need your help. I wasn't given a lot of technical knowledge concerning this structure, but I *do* know what it looks like." He pointed to the door. "If our orientation is correct and this is the crew cabin, that door can't exist. Do you agree?"

Ben thought for a moment and nodded. "That's an insulated wall," he said, focusing his attention. "Beyond that wall would be the edge."

"So, if we accept that at face value, this QET device leads to some corresponding location on Earth, and, from

180

our perspective it's simply painted onto the wall here."

Ben nodded. "Yeah, if you follow the logic, only the front face of the doorway is on this side. The other half is somewhere else. Might as well be a painting or a magic mirror."

"But you weren't the only one who described the hatchway we came in through as an 'escape' tube."

"Yeah, I guess I did. . . ."

"Why?"

He shrugged. "I don't know . . . "

"Could it be because that's what it actually is?" Railas suggested. "That implies that it's *not* the main entrance to this place." He tapped the wall with his metal fingers. "Think! This cabin is not the only part of this facility. If that was some sort of emergency regress, where would the main entrance be?"

"On the other side of the collectors where the control stations are," Woods answered for him.

"These are the quarters," Amy agreed. "This is where the parties would happen, but . . ."

"The workstations are in a smaller area towards the front scoop," Ben agreed. "There would be a main airlock there . . ."

"Which could be submerged just as this section is, but

it could also be far enough away to be above the surface."

"Hell Diver did tricks," Woods spoke up. "His rig was modified. Smelled like an old army boot inside, but he drove it in ways I'd never seen. His engines may be vacuum sealed. Maybe they could work in a fluid environment, or at least be able to float until he could dry them off . . ."

"Hell Diver is no friend of ours," Amy warned. "God knows how much Horgan *really* paid him, not just in money. The man sold his soul a long time ago."

"How would the crew get from quarters to the work area?" Railas demanded, looking at Ben.

"These facilities are usually pretty Spartan," he thought out loud. "There'd be a tunnel below the collectors."

"Back the way we came," Woods agreed.

Railas led the way back down the corridor into the main room, and finally to the curtain leading back to the entrance. The chamber was dimly lit, but they could easily make out where the flooring had been patched, covering another hatchway similar to the one above.

"He could have flooded that one, too," Woods warned.

"Not likely," Ben said. "The power generators and air

circulation would be controlled from down there. There'd be no seals that could be exposed to the outside, at least not directly."

"We could probably close the valves to the exit tunnel from there," Ben brightened. "There'd be pump controls in there, too. We could clear the tunnel and get back to the rig."

"Perhaps," Railas agreed. "But I'm inclined to think we'd find something more useful up ahead, such as that QEC system. Surely one of you could send a message to somebody on Earth who could make a difference."

"You guys are good at counting chickens," Woods scoffed. "Who's to say there's *anything* up there? I still think we should break down that other door. If it *does* lead to Earth, why not?"

"Where on Earth?" Railas asked. "You'd find yourself somewhere you're not familiar with, most likely a fortified domain controlled by your enemy. And you've already said they would kill you without hesitation rather than let you survive to tell about this. No, the surface of Titan is not a safe place, but it's *your* domain more than his." He looked to their faces. All agreed.

The tunnel was cramped; too low to stand upright in. There was a railing on either side and a ladder-like structure on the floor, as if the tunnel was intended to be set on an incline. Above them were large tanks and pipes that ran the length of the corridor with control stations placed strategically. Much of the equipment was not working and the warmth faded quickly from the air, causing them to don their breathers.

The corridor ended in a junction where they could stand up straight. A final door led forward, and Railas did not hesitate to work the valve, pulling the hatch open to reveal a spacious observation post. They stepped inside to see windows overlooking what would be the business end of the scoop and the airlock beyond. As Railas predicted, the airlock was only partially submerged, its door opening onto a sandbar. Waves of methane washed over the mouth of the airlock, but from the shore the structure might have appeared as nothing more than a natural outcropping. The glistening ice of a rig was just visible on the muddy horizon.

"How did we get this far?" Ben asked.

"I don't know," Railas admitted. "But it won't take long for somebody to realize we have. That ship should be able to hold us. Hopefully it has enough power to get back to the station."

But the airlock door opened before they could get to

it, and there stood the other shoe.

"T'hell are you doing here?" Boaz demanded. He stood comfortably in the low gravity of the scoop, wielding a long laser pistol. His armor made up for his frail form within and he faced them with a hard stare. Amy may have been right about his soul. His eyes were dark, whatever life may have previously been there long gone. He struck the barrel of his rifle against his armored hand. They were facing him on his home turf. He was an outsider used to living rough. And who were they to stop him?

Chapter Eighteen
Duel

Railas sized up Boaz, but he also made note of the open airlock. The room was intended for vehicles, which made it spacious, but Boaz had chosen to leave his outside. Why? Perhaps he had a solution for wading through liquid methane, or at least some means of navigating around the actual danger. He was surely used to the environment outside and his suit may even have been modified. Railas scolded himself. Beyond the door was micro gravity. A well-executed jump could land even a weak-kneed outsider several feet away, most likely beyond the worst of the lake. And keeping his rig outside provided an effective barrier for comparatively less skilled station dwellers.

"Who the hell even are you people?" Boaz demanded, glaring at them from inside his helmet. "I mean, I know you!" he shouted at Railas. "You're the new wind-up justice guy, right? Well, what does that make you, some kind of tin god?" He took a step forward. "So, what, are you here to arrest me? Try it!"

"Actually, yes I am," he said. "Somebody around here is guilty of more crimes than even *I* would have thought possible, and you're on the verge of committing more. Believe it or not, arresting you would be the kindest thing I could do for you right now."

"That a real laser rifle?" Ben asked, nodding at the weapon. "Where'd you get that?"

Boaz smiled, the servos in his arm barking and grinding as he wielded it for display. "The trick is not to bring a knife to a gunfight!"

"That's a real one all right," Woods confirmed. "I've only seen one other like that out here, and it wasn't as good–"

"The boss wants me to have the best," Boaz interrupted. He then angled the gun in their direction. "Back the way you came!"

Another clue. Yes, the laser rifle did look new, probably fresh off an assembly line on Earth. But his armor was not. Why would Horgan not fortify him with far better weaponry and more up-to-date defenses? Why was Boaz alone? Surely Horgan could have staffed his hideout with trained guards who didn't need motor-assisted armor to pass for mediocre. More puzzles. Something was not right.

Amy and Woods started to fall back, but Railas touched their arms to block them. Retreat was not the answer. He directed his gaze back at Boaz, his eyes brightening to scan for more details, but also perhaps to add emphasis to his next words. He took a step closer, and Boaz predictably singled him out with the gun.

Railas extended his palms, as if negotiating a truce. "Boaz . . . or Hell Diver if you really prefer, up until now you're only guilty of vice crimes and possible theft. After meeting your associate, I'm no longer clear on where you fit into the larger picture. But adding assault to the crimes I *do* know of won't help your case."

"Oh, you stupid tin bastard!" Boaz grumbled. "Why am I even talking to you?"

"Because I'm not afraid of you," he said. "And neither should they be."

Then, to add flair to his threat, Boaz adjusted the power cell, causing an almost imperceptible whine. It was not as effective as chambering a round would be in a more primitive weapon, but it was the best he could do.

"The problem, Mr. Boaz, is that everyone in this room is armor plated. These insulated suits are literally designed to dissipate heat. Yes, a sustained laser blast will eventually damage them, but it would take some pretty skillful shooting on your part. There's a reason why even energy weapons are not quite so common out here.

They're just not that practical."

"Bullets would be better," Ben agreed, following Railas's lead. "A good shotgun blast would go through one of these suits, but you'd need a bigger heat gun than that to do the same job with a single jolt."

Boaz glanced down at his gun, his mind now confused.

"You could shoot *me*," Railas admitted, "but you'd have to know what you were doing. As a robot, I feel no pain. A laser can heat up my components, but many of them are designed for extreme temperatures. Also, much of my chassis is airspace and my critical systems are well protected. You may damage me, I'll admit, but I doubt you could actually stop me before I disarm you, especially if I don't stand still."

"I'll open the door!" he threatened.

"Better," Railas agreed. "But, again, we're all dressed for the cold, even you."

"What's he paying you?" Amy spoke up. "What could he *possibly* be paying you?"

At this, Boaz snickered. And something about his expression made even Woods uncomfortable. Whatever Boaz was, he was not redeemable by them. And then he made his move.

The first laser blast hit Ben, thermo-shocking the plate on his chest and causing it to crackle. But, as Railas predicted, Ben had time to move before the damage became severe. Woods, on the other hand, reacted far less strategically. He ran at Boaz with the same clumsy anger he'd unleashed so unsuccessfully on Railas. He even roared, effectively announcing his charge. And, though Boaz was far from skillful, he had enough luck to get off another shot, this one more successful.

The laser charge hit Woods' breather, melting the components into a polymer soup, which burned his face and made the unit ineffective. Woods cried out in pain, peeling the face plate off and running for the airlock door. Railas took advantage of the confusion and jumped forward, gripping the rifle hard with his hands. Boaz danced skillfully in the low gravity and landed a vicious kick on Railas's knee, a move that would have been far more effective against even an armored human, but to a robot, now secured magnetically to the metal floor, it was meaningless.

Boaz squirmed on the floor, his foot having taken the brunt of the blow even through his armor. And, though he still fought to topple Railas, his under-developed leg muscles were unable to shift him even with the help of his servos. While he continued to try to seize the gun, Ben struck him hard on the side of the head, half dislodging his helmet.

Boaz danced away, shouting curses at Ben as he adjusted the helmet with his hands. Had Boaz's armor plating not been more combative than Ben's, the fight would have been completely over. He reached behind his back, perhaps rummaging for another weapon. But Railas still had the rifle and he crouched, taking aim.

"Unlike you, I could track your movement more accurately and update my aim as you move," Railas warned. "I could carve a portrait of you in the wall faster than you could put one hole in a stationary target. If necessary, I could render your life support system useless or weaken your armor in critical areas."

"So that's how it is?" he groaned.

Railas nodded. "Yes, that's how it is."

Amy emerged from the airlock door. "Nate's hurt pretty bad," she warned.

"Can he walk?" Railas asked.

"Yeah."

"Give him your breather," Railas told Boaz.

"You don't ask a man for that!" he said, putting his hands on his hips.

"In this case I do." He turned to Ben. "Can you fly that rig?"

"Yeah, I think so," he said with moderate confidence.

"I'll need you to take Amy and Nathan back to Shangri-La and report what you've seen here. I'll deal with Hell Diver and Mr. Horgan."

"No way," Ben said. "They'll kill you!"

"Maybe," Railas admitted. "But let me ask you something: How did Horgan know Mr. Woods by name? I'll bet he knew you as well. How?"

"Is that important now?"

"I think it is," Railas said. "He knew we were coming, he must have. He could have stopped us, but he didn't. This was some kind of game, just like Woods said, and I need to know where it ends."

"That's kind of farfetched," Ben disagreed. "And, even if it's true, it makes you even *more* dangerous to them. They will kill you," he repeated.

"They may *destroy* me," Railas corrected him. "But you're still in greater danger. So is everyone else, particularly people like Mindy. If I can document what I've seen here, my memory may be useful as evidence. Even a few moments near a communication console would allow me to broadcast critical information."

"Assuming they let you . . ."

"No!" Boaz screamed, his voice taking on the whining tone of a disappointed child. "It's not the way you think, you robot bastard! *You're* the intruder here, you always were! And there's no way you're gonna ruin things for me. You're not taking my ride . . . We weren't going to hurt her . . . What's her name?" He indicated Amy.

"So *you* don't know their names," Railas commented. "Or you want me to *believe* you don't. Which is it? Do you remember Mindy?"

He looked confused. "I'm not what you think! I'm supposed to be the hero!"

"Where's Mindy?" Railas demanded.

"Who?"

Railas paused, leaving an uncomfortable silence, processing his lack of an answer as an answer. He turned to Ben. "Getting Amy back to safety has to be your priority. I'll let no harm come to her, and you're the only one who can get her back." Then he turned to Boaz. "Your boss is not a good man, Mr. Hell Diver. You would have done better to cooperate with us when you could. Now it's too late. Give Ben your breather and wait in the substation until they leave. Then we'll talk to Horgan together. And I'm now quite certain that you *are* exactly what we think you are. Or worse."

But then, like a cornered animal, Boaz lashed out once again, this time leaping back towards the outer door. Then he carried out his threat. The door began to cycle open, bringing in the cold, murky atmosphere from outside.

And then, like a pirate wannabe, Boaz let out a screeching laugh and ran about the room, timing a rehearsed jump to get him out the door, over the receding waves, and onto the sand bar when the door was just high enough for him to clear it. Railas ran after him, mimicking his leap across the glistening pool. But, either because of his weight or subtleties in balance, he came up short, planting his feet several inches into the salty alien mud. He sensed extreme cold, and he could hear his polymer skin crackle as he moved. His power systems were slowing quickly and he wondered about his battery efficiency. His servos were becoming sticky and his joints were showing signs of seizing. He had seconds or very few minutes. But he was not going the let Boaz have the rig. That would leave Amy in Horgan's hands, as well as the others.

He could still see, but was having difficulty positioning his head. Boaz was already approaching the ship, and he would be able to operate it very quickly. If he got in he would be gone. Railas's knees almost bound as he crouched, and his servos were complaining. He disconnected all power governors and safety locks before parts of his system shut down. Then he did a second leap, this time aiming himself directly at Boaz.

The two collided as Boaz reached for the door, similar to the bubble cockpit hatch of their own rig. The door popped opened on its huge hinges, but Boaz found himself underneath the rig as he struggled with Railas, the cold mud packing into the joints of his suit. But something worse had happened. Both his legs were broken where Railas's metal frame had struck him, their knee joints shattered and the armor destroyed. His long-lost bone density was unable to protect him, and whatever remained of his knees would likely be unsalvageable. Why he didn't succumb to the obvious pain he must be in was another mystery. Perhaps his nerves and muscles had atrophied along with his bones or he was under the influence of adrenalin and drugs. He gripped savagely at the rig's skis trying to pull himself away from Railas, who could not speak usefully in the cold, thick air, his speakers now encased in dry ice.

But then Boaz treated them to one more surprise. His

last act of defiance was to operate a hidden switch within his chest plate. Something popped in the rear of his armor. A panel flew off and something burst forth, looking surprisingly like a parachute opening for a sky diver. A great balloon inflated, immediately catching the wind and carrying Boaz away!

Railas stared after him briefly as Amy and Ben approached, carrying Woods in tow between them. Railas passed them on his way back into the airlock, sealing it behind him and cycling the air circulators to bring in what comparative warmth he could. Unlike the rig they'd arrived in, Hell Diver's contraption did not have a rear compartment. Railas would not have been able to fit even if he'd chosen to go with them. As it was, the three of them would be hard pressed to find room in the bubble for comfort. But the door could close, and that's all that mattered. Within moments, Ben had the engines started. Railas watched as the craft rose into the air and out of immediate sight.

Satisfied, he made his way back down the tunnel to the warm room beyond. It was time to face Mr. Horgan. By the time he reached the strange door, his speaker system would be thawed. He would have his answers.

Chapter Nineteen
Doorway

Railas searched his feelings as his feet clunked on floor of the metal tunnel. He was angry, but he didn't know why. Horgan had orchestrated the nightmares he suspected took place in the substation, but he had also done far worse. He had used everyone, from the station governor to Rittenhouse, and everyone who worked under them. Even his stooge, Hell Diver, was cast aside when he was no longer needed. And he'd tried to use Railas as well. No more! The pain he'd caused these people was beyond understanding. Pain and fear. He'd seen it in their eyes, starting with his first meeting with Amy. And it all came from Horgan. Those in the Sandbox were afraid. Gibbs, the security chief, was afraid to do his job. And even Halloran was only a superior pawn himself. Everyone was expendable including Mindy, who he was still determined to find. But under that was something worse, something he couldn't yet identify. Something perhaps so obvious he couldn't see it.

He pondered. Humans had complicated minds, often

working at cross purposes with themselves and each other. And they seldom connected critical dots, particularly when doing so would reveal things they didn't want to believe. They looked without seeing. Was that happening to him as well? His thought process was more ordered, but not so unlike that of a human mind. And, like a human, he had no choice but to proceed and let his mind work itself out as more data became available.

Nobody waited for him at the entry way or the main room. He had expected some kind of reception. Perhaps they actually believed he'd fled the facility with the others or that he'd be hopelessly marooned in the substation. He looked down at himself in the warm light of the room. The plastic skin had been reduced to sticky ooze and his plates were badly discolored. The salty mud had impacted his joints and was leaving a trail of dust behind him as it ground free from his bearings and solenoids. Otherwise he was functional, though it would take time to completely restore his range of movement and to clean and lubricate his servos.

The door that shouldn't have been there was still closed, and could not easily be opened from this side. But Railas had brought the laser rifle and it was still charged. He aimed it at the most likely place for the latch to be and pulled the trigger. The power pack made a whining sound when charging, but the actual discharge was silent. He could sense the power transfer, but nothing beyond that. The door glowed red. It was fortified, but not impregnable. Once the metal was soft enough, a good kick would be all that was required, and his magnetic feet allowed him to deliver a great deal of force. The kick itself didn't even make that much noise. And then he stepped through.

Confusion. Yes, he felt an immediate difference in gravity and environment, but there was something else. Something unexpected. As he stepped through, *everything* shifted. And, unlike any expectations he might have had concerning quantum entanglement transport, the door disappeared behind him. And then he knew where he was.

The yellow room! The floor was cold and even, and the gravity was not like he remembered. It was Earth normal. But something about the lighting brought out details he'd not previously seen. This was the same yellow room he'd started in, but yet it wasn't. Something very profound had happened.

The door opened, and somehow Railas had expected it to. In came Rittenhouse, his suit well pressed and his tie straight. Behind him, looking sheepish, was Amy Noise.

"Well now," Rittenhouse began, mimicking the manner of a busy doctor on rounds. "How do you feel, Railas? That download must have been pretty intense. Did you experience any unusual sensations? Any memories you can't account for?"

"Of course," Railas said. "Now I understand." He looked down at his legs, finding no traces of ruined plastic or discoloration, nor was there any salty mud residue in his joints. He looked from Rittenhouse's face to Amy's.

"Where do you think you are?" Rittenhouse asked.

He shook his head. "I suppose you want me to say that I took a trip to Earth through a quantum entanglement tunnel, but somehow that was a dream, or the equivalent. But I suspect it's the opposite."

Rittenhouse nodded.

"But this was not a memory download either."

Rittenhouse looked surprised. "Why would you think that?"

"Because you expected me to believe this was the same room I originally awakened in, and I know it's not."

He shrugged. "How would you know that?"

"You forget the nature of my memory. While it's true that my personal recollections can be subjective, I still retain much more detail. I can compare images I see now with those I saw before. I remember this room having far less imperfections in its surfaces. The patterns in the stone blocks, for example, were less detailed, and the textures themselves not as unique, but repeated like wallpaper. The same is true of color variations. The differences are subtle but numerous, though I didn't notice them before. I suspect the eyes you upgraded me to see better than you thought. All of this was some kind of simulation, wasn't it?"

"I'm sorry, Railas," Amy whispered.

"At least you're safe," Railas said. "So am I, by the way, but I shouldn't have been. That's what I was missing." He regarded Amy. "When I chased Boaz across the lake my intention was to prevent him from escaping with your only available transport. Doing so exposed me to the atmosphere and the extreme cold. As expected, I suffered condensation and frost action in my joints and servos, which probably would have frozen them completely, now that I think of it. What was missing, however, were similar issues with my boards and critical systems. I doubt I could have remained functional under those circumstances. Memory would have failed, and I could have expected processor errors and battery shorts. But I suffered no permanent damage at all."

"The simulation was real time," Rittenhouse explained. "We tried to stay ahead of you, but we never expected you to go outside. We'd assumed you'd choose the doorway, as you ultimately did. We never finished programming the kind of damage you would have experienced on the surface." He smiled. "You were never supposed to jump into that methane pool. We assumed you wouldn't try. Statistically, it should have been safer and more advantageous for you to remain operational and take the fight back to Horgan even if that would be riskier for Amy. Honestly, we never expected you to willingly risk your life for her, Ben, and even Nathan!"

"I'm glad I entertained you so much."

"But you're missing the point!" Rittenhouse said, dancing with enthusiasm. "You actually showed literal human heroism! Passion! Loyalty! We still don't know how that's even possible! We could never have predicted any of this!"

"So now, like my mysterious hardware anomalies, you still maintain that you don't know exactly how I work?"

"Not completely, no," Rittenhouse admitted. "When your consciousness was just a program none of this was apparent. Somehow the incorporation of the software with your Robo-Naut hardware must have done something . . ."

"What happened to Mindy?" he asked Rittenhouse.

He shook his head. "Mindy was the first problem. You see, I was connected to the simulation, experiencing it with you as my character, so was Amy here . . ."

"There *was* no Mindy," Amy said, her gaze not meeting his. "She was just a story I told you. She never really existed as a character."

"Railas, you're magnificent!" Rittenhouse said, completely ignoring Amy and what was exchanged between them. "This whole program was supposed to be a lot simpler, but we couldn't keep up with you! Not even close! You obsessed over details we never thought you'd see as important and you followed leads that didn't even exist! All you were supposed to do is prove you could litigate. We never expected you to become a hero."

"And I suppose the real Shangri-La –"

"Oh, for heaven's sake, it's a VR game!" he laughed. "You're connected now, go see for yourself! Go access the game! It's actually called 'Hell Diver!' You should see it."

Railas dared to look through the network, searching for the appropriate key words. Images appeared of the station, the bubble-like rigs cavorting around in the fog, and the excited faces of adventurers. Here Boaz was featured as a pirate-like character, whose exaggerated face made up part of the game logo. The simplified version of the station was only a setting for various simulated trades, feuds, and deals. On a whim, Railas reached out for actual images of Titan, seeing the rough terrain where the station would have been and the methane lake that held the nonexistent substation. But no landings had actually happened there, and no permanent structures existed. None of it was real, not even as a plan. Only a fantasy.

"We bought the rights to the game," Rittenhouse boasted. "But we modified it considerably to use as our testing ground. We hired the characters, mostly gamers with ambition . . ."

"The Sandbox was not part of the game," Amy said. "It was like a break room where the gamers could chat on their own. Some of them weren't even in the game as regular characters. Some were just extras or observers. Nobody understood what was going on when you showed up there."

"The term 'sandbox' is sometimes used for a designated area to test or try out various tools," Railas understood.

Rittenhouse nodded. "All that because some idiot, while writing a spreadsheet you were never supposed to read, put a decimal in the wrong place and made Boaz look like a millionaire instead of just a petty crook."

"Some of the people you interacted with also added more details than they were supposed to," Amy explained. "I think McClusky fancied herself some kind of junior programmer. She thought your being there was a training simulation for improvisation. She ended up creating a whole new story line by accident."

"Got that right!" Rittenhouse laughed. "That fool ended up changing the entire game board! We had coders working day and night creating all that extra stuff! That whole substation thing was never supposed to lead anywhere. It was just a diagram, for heaven's sake! We had to design that place overnight as well as get you into an actual rig! Didn't even make real sense! No way one of those rigs could carry or even shift something that large anyway. The QET was another load of crap we made up on the fly. You were supposed to come to Earth that way, where you were all along, and we'd transition you into *this* reality. Looks like you were just too smart for us."

Railas scanned the room. "Well, now that you've run your test, what happens next?"

"Now we do it for real!" Rittenhouse exclaimed, grasping his hands. "Now we apply our theories of justice reform to *actual* cases here on Earth. And that's just the beginning!"

"Are you insane?" Railas shouted. "If I've proven anything to you through all of this, it should be that you can't trust me to play by the ridiculous and ever-changing rules you humans manage to create. I wouldn't be loyal to your Horgan, Halloran, or even *you* in the long run!"

"Nor should you be," Rittenhouse said. "That was the point all along!"

There was a pause in which Railas studied their expressions. Amy was solemn and even Rittenhouse seemed far more serious than usual.

"Our society is at a turning point right now," Rittenhouse said with a sigh. "We've got factions trying to divide up our nations and our world. And they've been known to criminalize politics. They even use institutions like the police and the courts to punish those they don't like while helping those they do. Even the highest courts in our land are not safe."

"And we also have PACE," Amy added, and something in her voice denoted fear, the very same fear that had been there all along.

"An automation company?"

"People are using technology to watch us and control

us. We're losing our freedom. *We* need to use technology to fight back."

"That's where you come in," Rittenhouse said. "You're truly impartial. That's what we need. Somebody to watch the watchers, somebody who *can't* be bought or threatened!"

"And you're good," Amy emphasized. "You're decent and honest. You actually cared about us. You even cared about Mindy, somebody you never even met."

Rittenhouse opened the door again, this time revealing daylight in the corridor beyond. He took Railas's hand and led him outside, guiding him to a great window at the end of the hall. They were not in a basement, as he'd been led to believe, but in an upper floor of a skyscraper overlooking a city he didn't bother to identify. He looked down at the traffic, picking out individual people moving about on their various journeys. The sky was bright and clear, lighting up their faces.

"You're the hope of the world, Railas," Rittenhouse said, resting his hand on his shoulder. "You'll be the first of many, hopefully. But we need you, my friend. We still have no idea how you work. I wasn't kidding about that. We can't easily re-create you. The initial transfer was the only one that worked. You were first downloaded into the

Robo-Naut because PACE was –"

"There was a complication," Amy said. "We've been trying to unravel it ever since. We had to re-start you a few times. We don't know exactly what happened to cause this . . . effect."

Rittenhouse nodded. "We don't know why your processing ability exceeds your processors . . ."

"But it does," Amy said. "It was my idea to switch the feed from your sensors to the VR system during your activation, but even that was hit or miss. Now at least we know who you are, and that we can really trust you. We have the full record of your story."

A sound issued from Railas that resembled a laugh, his first ever. "The same kind of memory record I would have used to save you on Titan. An Irony that it now saves me *from* you, from you destroying all that I remember, false though it is. From another deactivation and reset cycle."

Amy's face took on shame. "Railas, you have my word, we'll *never* do that again. We don't *need* to now."

Railas didn't bother to comment. Instead, he looked again at the vehicles, the walkways, and the windows of the other buildings. It might have been a malfunction, but he wondered about Mindy. Part of his mind couldn't believe even now that she was only a name in the backstory of another character, not even interesting enough to be featured in the game itself. Something about that seemed wrong and cruel. He alone would remember Mindy, whether she was real or not. He would preserve her memory forever, as long as he lived, though he didn't know why. Perhaps the idea of being erased gave them something in common. Who knows how many times he'd been forced to forget her.

Would he do what they asked? Would he accept their explanations? They had lied to him since the beginning. Every memory he had up to that point had been based on a lie, and they weren't telling him everything now. Even Amy was hiding more. He believed part of what they said, however. He believed that they didn't understand how he worked. They hadn't created him. They could re-create his activation, but not his installation. The proof was in his first command. "Railas." That was the command code they were modifying each time. He could see the remains of several versions of it, all in the same directory. And it replaced another code they had tried to delete altogether. When he attempted to access it he got no details, but there was an impression left, an echo of something else. The accident that installed his program was *not* an accident.

And he was not unique. There was at least one other.

Please enjoy my free gift for reading this book!

Join my mailing list and you will receive a free copy of Twisted Fire, a short story anthology! Please go to the following link for details:

www.pauljosephbooks.com/land.html

Paul J. Joseph is an independent film maker as well as a storyteller through writing. One of his films was featured in the 2010 Ava Gardner Independent Film Festival. He has been teaching mass communication courses at a college level for 25 years and currently works at a small private university in North Carolina. He lives with his wife Tyreese, his son Ian, a mother in law, and three cats.

If you have enjoyed this book, please take a moment to write a review on Bookbub, Goodreads, Amazon, or other retailers.

Continue your journey with **The Railas Verdict**

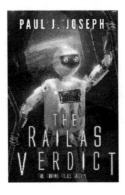

The Railas Verdict: Elevator to the Stars!

Everything in New Braintree was efficient, comfortable, and convenient, but tightly controlled by PACE, a technology provider with dark ambitions of global dominance. Their proposed justice robot, MAX, is more of a politician than a judge and lacks even simulated ethics. Railas, now fully operational, is the only alternative. He cannot be intimidated or bribed, and he was created to work against tyranny. His team has high hopes to restore justice and defeat PACE. But while Railas and his team investigate MAX and his motives, he finds something worse. His mysterious creator, who vanished from her office on the space elevator, makes a surprise appearance in VR. Her digital essence, coupled with something far away, may represent an unimaginable threat.

To enjoy other titles in this series by Paul J. Joseph, look for the following: All are available on Amazon.com

The Turing Files

Book 1 Romo's Journey

Book 2 Romo's World

Book 3 The Railas Project

Book 4 The Railas Verdict

Book 5 Romo's Return

Book 6 Romo's Mission

Through the Fold Series

Book 1 Marker Stone

Book 2 Homesick

Book 3 Web of Life

Book 4 Splashdown

Book 5 Infinity Machine

Book 6 Window in the Sky

Contact me on Facebook at **Paul J Joseph Author** or

Visit my website at **www.pauljosephbooks.com**

Join my **mailing list** for updates!

Made in the USA
Middletown, DE
07 November 2021

51803564R00128